MAMBO TO MURDER

BY CHARLENE TORKELSON

Copyright © 2011 Charlene Torkelson
All rights reserved.
ISBN: 0615476058
ISBN-13: 9780615476056

This book is dedicated to all the dancers I have met, all the dancers I have danced with, and all those I have taught. In some form or another you are a part of this book. A piece of you is in each and every character and in each dance performed. You are a special group of people with unique talents. You have and always will be a part of my life. Since the first year I began ballroom dancing, I have worn a small gold band on my little finger signifying my dedication and connection to all the dancers in the world. This book is for all of you who have played such a significant role in my life. Thank you.

INTRODUCTION:

Festival! That magical time of year when the dance studios in Minneapolis were transformed into gala parties with colorful décor. When costumes and celebration enticed new dancers to venture into the studio for nights of music and merriment, and continuing dancers tried out their moves to the delight of their teachers. And when dance teachers showed off their expertise and showmanship for their fellow professionals. Festival! Six weeks of anticipated enchantment.

The year was 1976 and the theme of this celebration was "Broadway". Amid the excitement and festive mood, the highlight would be the "West Side Story" party when the Jets gang from the Minneapolis city area would rival the Sharks from the suburb studio in a dance-off. Cool and collected, the staff from Minneapolis entered the arena – the polished wooden dance floor perimeter crowded with costumed students waiting anxiously for the music to strike a first beat. It hit and the dancers in blue jeans, white t-shirts and slicked back hair performed a lively jive. As the crowd clapped wildly, the rival Sharks entered – dressed in black with vivid hot pinks and reds as accents – they ended the challenge with a fast and exciting Mambo. The Mambo would win hands down. The enticing Latin hip motion and crisp spins made even the non-believers swoon with delight. Viva la Mambo!

Later it would be called the Mambo to Murder or the Mambo of Death because in spite of the friendly banter between these two rival "gangs", at the end of the evening there would be an actual body – a murder victim similar to the end of the Broadway version of "West Side Story" except this time it wasn't acting. This time it was real.

I.

The 1950's had been a showcase dance decade for the city of Minneapolis. Angelo D'Lario owned and operated one of the premier buildings along Hennepin Avenue. Tall and classic with its brick exterior and valet entrance, D'Lario's dance studio had been the center of entertainment for the rich and powerful until the day it was closed down. D'Lario was charged with tax evasion and sent to prison. Although tax charges were his downfall, his business was clearly more than dancing and taxes were the compromised charges brought against him just to shut down the other parts of his operation. Needless to say, the dance world in the city was clouded with a wall of distrust, deception, and fraud that wouldn't be touched again for another decade when a young but charismatic dancer named Edward Garrett once again tried to revive its image. That sinful wall would come tumbling down.

Edward Garrett would open his tiny studio beneath a parking ramp in the heart of the business district. As the busy world of business executives and secretaries parked their cars and rode down the elevator to their concrete existence of nine to five, the world of dance opened up there right at the end of their journey – enticing. The windows facing the elevator door were graced with sheer curtains waving slightly to reveal the glossy wooden dance floor beyond, filled with music and graceful couples. Each day as these young clerics passed, one or two would stop and watch or even venture in to inquire how they too could move like the man or woman out there on that floor. Soon, the studio became a bustling business again. Edward Garrett would spend his entire career building the reputation of dancing and its benefits to this skeptical community. It would once again be lifted to a profession of respect.

Not to say that Edward was without faults. No, that certainly could not be said at all. In fact, Edward Garrett was perhaps one of the most complicated individuals anyone could ever encounter. He had excitement and vitality. Where ever he went, he was the center of attention. Women were drawn to him. And he was drawn to them. Unfortunately for most, Edward was not one who remained monogamous for long if at all. Men were drawn to him as well in spite of the fact that any man with a wife or girlfriend soon found himself alone when Edward was in attendance. The women practically swarmed all over him begging for a chance to hit the floor for just one song in his masterful arms. A good dancer with a charming personality can't lose. That was the message Edward presented. Men realized soon enough that message was clear. The studio was filled not only with good looking women, but with men who wanted to have what Edward Garrett had.

Edward Garrett sat moodily in his overstuffed office chair. In spite of his corner office opening to a perfect view of the dance floor and arena he had built for himself, his curtained windows were usually shrouded and closed. He had called in his trio of upper management staff. Dennis Whit was thin and wiry with a talent for dancing that was a thorn in Edward's side most of the time. Suzanna Caldwell was tiny and birdlike – clearly not the kind of woman Edward felt should be a dancer. His ideal woman was tall and lanky with a perfect model-like appearance. Suzanna's small pinched face and large owl glasses disguised the fact that she was an incredible dancer and technician. Mary Lou Smith was outspoken and crisp – a take charge person who found the rivalry between the three to be stimulating and exciting.

As usual, Edward and Dennis were butting heads. Edward slumped in his chair and glared at Dennis.

"I'm ready to move on," Dennis had said. Mr. Whit had been with the studio for six years since he was just out of high school. He didn't look now as if he was any older than eighteen. His slight wisp of a mustache had been growing for weeks and his gangly limbs reminded Edward of the scarecrow in the Wizard of Oz. His dance ability also rivaled that movie scarecrow with his agility and limber movements. He was a showman, there was no doubt about it.

"Move on? To where? I own the territory rights for two hundred fifty miles in all directions. That's what your contract clearly states. You'd end up in a cornfield in Iowa or in the frozen tundra of Canada if you tried to open a studio out of that circle. Good luck!" Edward snorted with a haughty laugh.

"Well, then it's on to the corn fields, I guess," Dennis flung right back. "Anything to get away from you and your dictator mentality. How I worked for you this long is a wonder to me."

"I taught you everything you know. You owe me!" bellowed Edward. "Just try and make it without me. I dare you."

Well, that was the wrong thing to say at that moment because with Edward's final taunt Dennis rose from his chair and ambled out the door. Then he ambled right out the front door. Edward Garrett for a moment opened his mouth to call out, but just as quickly shut it and leaned back into his favorite pouting position. His cheeks puffed out and his lower lip stuck out as he nervously tapped his heels up and down on the floor causing his knees to flutter like a hyperactive preschooler.

Mary Lou Smith sat back and began to smile. One less person to compete with. Another piece of the pie for her. This was good – very good indeed. Now was the time to hit him with her latest great idea for success.

"Mr. Garrett," she purred softly. "Maybe it's time to open another studio here – a second one. One in a suburb. There is plenty of wealth and money in the suburbs. Those people are just waiting for a dance studio and aren't likely to venture downtown. They live 'out there' and they play 'out there'. Now is the time to hit. It could be huge!"

Edward leaned back in his chair. His pouting face softened. He pondered the thought and then nodded. "Maybe."

II.

A month later they were considering which wealthy suburb would house the new studio. All votes were in with proposals and building plans laid out on Edward Garrett's large cherry desktop. Mary Lou Smith was pointing out the possibilities and the pros and cons for each location. Edward was lost in thought as he half heartedly listened. He missed Dennis Whit more than he had imagined but the indignity of his walk out also fueled the drive to compete and succeed in this venture. He needed not only to prove something to Mr. Whit but also to himself. He was the king of dance in this area, and a new studio would cement that crown. It was a matter of pride. His mind wandered back to Mary Lou droning on about a place in Edina, a wealthy suburb.

"Let's do this one," he pointed to her proposal for a large spacious storefront in a strip mall across from a prominent shopping area. It was visible and the area was crowded with suburbanites just waiting for a place to learn to dance the latest fad dances. Disco was about to break open and clubs would be opening up quickly once it hit. It was time to strike now.

Edward supervised every inch of the remodeling. The downtown studio was quiet and subdued with basic colors and a quiet elegance. This new studio would be just the opposite. The walls were splashed with vibrant paper that screamed "disco fever". The eye popping shiny finish of each contrasting wall was hard to miss from the hallway. The large front desk was carpeted up the sides in the same teal carpet that striped across the reception area ending at the small ballroom's wooden planks. That in turn provided a straight walkway to the large ballroom in the back of the space. With no windows or natural light poring in like the downtown studio, this studio was more like a large closed off barn. Edward's primitive art collection and glistening mirrors were the brightness that replaced the sunlight. It was faddish and would draw attention immediately.

Again, Edward's personal office was off the reception area. With its own circling silver patterned walls, it was eye popping and vibrant. Clean with crisp new décor, it would prove to be another useless space as Edward would rarely venture out to this studio once it opened. He was a city dweller, living in a top story condo behind his original studio space. He rarely drove any place unless absolutely necessary. Instead he frequented the many clubs and shops in the immediate downtown area mingling with the "beautiful" people. Of course he would have a gala grand opening and invite all of those fabulous trendy downtowners out to the suburbs. They would be amazed at his taste and flare for the contemporary. His mind was wandering to that event and how incredible it would be. Now just to decide which staff members would service this new studio.

The downtown studio housed about twenty teachers, executives, and trainees. It was a busy and active place with everyone – students included – interacting to create a pleasant atmosphere. If you happened to come into the studio frustrated from a busy and tiring day at work, that mood would soon change. The laughter, music and activity had everyone giddy. It was truly contagious. By the end of the day, people left with a whistle and a song as well as a lightness in their step.

The only thing that could cloud that mood was a sullen Edward Garrett. Edward was stuck in his habits and his expectations. He expected everyone to be beautiful, professional, and perfect. That meant calling each other by their last names as in "Miss" so-and so or "Mr." so-and so. First names were not allowed. Women teachers were to wear dresses, skirts, pantyhose and heels. There were no exceptions. Their make up was to be applied with a professional hand before stepping out on the dance floor. Anyone caught with no lipstick would be promptly sent back to the teachers' office to apply a fresh coat. Men were to be dressed in freshly pressed suits and ties. Bow ties were acceptable if suited to the rest of their attire. Hair was always expected to be current in style. Many a time Edward would single out some poor soul in the daily meeting who needed a hair cut or could shed a few pounds. Tears were not uncommon during meeting time. But once the rest of the day started, the smiles were right back on every face. Yes, Edward could be a hurricane on a sunny day, but he couldn't keep the mood down for long.

Behind his back, Mr. Garrett was referred to as "Eddie G". Did he know about the nickname? No one knew for sure. If he did, he never mentioned it. Eddie G was never on time for anything. In fact, he banned clocks from the studio. That way, he must have told himself, no one would know that he was late. The receptionist would set a timer to start the lesson hour and when that timer rang again, the lessons would end. That was called Eddie G time.

Today the meeting was short and sweet. Edward Garrett sat in the front of the group with a Howdy Doody smile ready to announce his choices for the new studio staff. There would be four teachers chosen – two women and two men – in addition to one executive staff member.

He first announced the two women: Charlotte Papalo and Becca Fine. Then the two men: Lee Watkins and Kenneth Andrews. Charlotte seemed very pleased as did the two men. Becca fidgeted a bit but then cheerfully took her spot next to the others as they stood before the remaining staff.

"I am pleased to announce that the executive in charge of our new studio will be...drum roll please!" Edward made his grand announcement special by allowing the remaining staff to drum roll on the table tops. "Miss Charlotte Papalo!"

Charlotte let go an excited gasp as Mary Lou Smith jumped to her feet and demanded Edward Garrett reconsider and make her the studio manager. "This whole thing was my plan – my idea. How dare you give my position to someone else! I need to meet with you immediately. Your office, let's go!"

Poor Charlotte looked as if she had just received a swift kick to the stomach. Her face went ashen and she doubled over in a whimper. This was hardly the reaction she had anticipated when she first heard the news. And of course, that was what it was, a new and startling piece of news. Charlotte was a waif of a woman with large brown eyes and a heart shaped face framed by long locks of golden brown hair. Her dancing was her strength, and

Edward's attentions to her because of her beauty and sweetness were always evident.

Mary Lou Smith on the other hand was small in stature, square, and business like with short tightly curled hair and sensible shoes. She was also a pit bull when it came to issues she felt were important to the studio. She was a real go-getter who could produce results. This was obviously one of those "important issues". She stalked into Edward's office with a defiant Eddie G following. No one knew what was said in that office behind the closed door, but when it was over, Edward Garrett came out to announce that indeed he had been "mistaken" and Mary Lou Smith would be the manager of the new studio with Charlotte Papalo as her "assistant".

Needless to say, the excitement that had just filled the studio before that meeting was now dust – a cloud of frustration, anger, and confusion. Charlotte actually looked a bit relieved. After all, managing a studio for Edward Garrett would be no picnic. In fact it was probably one of the worst scenarios anyone who worked for the man could ever imagine. No one could live up to the perfection Edward demanded. That is unless you were a pit bull like Mary Lou Smith who didn't really care what Edward thought at all.

III.

Mary Lou Smith sat in her new office admiring her view of the dance floor. She had a photo of her dog propped on her desk in a frame decorated with tiny bones. She smiled as she gazed out across the glossy floor to the front desk so new and fresh. This had been her dream and now it was all coming true. Sure, there were no students yet. But the Grand Opening would be tomorrow night when all the dignitaries, staff and upper crust wealthy from the area would be introduced to the studio. Then it would be a hot bed of activity and students aplenty. She couldn't wait.

"Parker!" she bellowed across the dance floor to the front desk. Eloise Parker was a downtown student who lived out in this area and had taken the job as receptionist in exchange for a small salary and continuing dance lessons. Former students always wanted to be a part of the studio as a staff member – that is until they actually became a part of the staff. Then they saw it wasn't all fun and games as they had pictured in their minds.

Eloise Parker peeked over the top of the too tall desk to see what Miss Smith was yelling about. "Parker! Come here!" Mary Lou Smith bellowed again.

Eloise quickly stood and scampered across the slick floor skidding every which way as she scooted. She was a middle aged woman with thinning mousey blond hair and a lopsided puffy face who wanted to remain young. Actually, everything about her suggested that she thought she was young. She dressed in short skirts and too tight sweaters and wore shoes that were too tall for her in an attempt to give her short body that long legged look. Her lipstick always bled over her actual lip lines so it looked like a clown had applied her makeup. Her eyes were heavily made up even though it made the creases around her eyes look like dried up river beds. She didn't seem to notice as long as she was up on the latest fads. "You called, Miss Smith?"

"Yes, I did. Where is the guest list for our grand opening tomorrow? Did the downtown studio send it out yet?" Mary Lou demanded.

"Not yet. I haven't seen one yet...", Eloise stammered.

"Well, call down there and get something sent out immediately. Immediately you understand?" Mary Lou's voice echoed in the large empty room.

Eloise nodded and quickly scampered back to the refuge of the too tall desk to make a phone call. She tried

14

to whisper into the phone as every little noise seemed to reverberate through the empty rooms.

The name Mary Lou Smith seemed all so common. That is what all her students used to say when they first heard it. "That's because my name is really Louella Findlesmith. Way too long. So I shortened it to Mary Lou Smith," she would say with a twinkle in her eye. They would all laugh at her joke. The only thing was it wasn't really a joke at all. It was true. She was really Louella Findlesmith, but Edward Garrett had immediately suggested she change it. "Too long and forgettable" he had said. And it was. But Mary Lou Smith seemed too common. Oh well, she had thought. The name served her well. It was something one remembered.

Charlotte Papalo sauntered into the studio. She wasn't one to hold a grudge so waved a friendly well manicured hand in Mary Lou's direction as she stopped at the front desk to greet Eloise. Charlotte was pencil thin except for large firm breasts that usually showed prominently in whatever she wore. Her clothes were – well, different. They swayed, they floated, and they shimmered. She always chose something unusual with an underlying sensual feel. Today she wore a peach wrapped skirt with a pair of white leggings underneath. She wore several layers of tops starting with a skinny white tube top covered with a flower patterned peach and beige wrapped jacket with winged sleeves. She wore flat beaded sandals and carried a pair of three inch heeled gold dance shoes. Over her shoulder slung a large cloth bag of gray canvas with black leather straps edging the opening and bottom. Viewing the small ballroom for the first time, she wandered around stopping at each mirror to admire the spaciousness it provided. She fingered the doorway to the teachers' office admiring the cleanness and freshness of the lines. Then she entered the long narrow office space to change her shoes.

Lee Watkins, one of the male teachers chosen for the new studio, came in seconds later. He grinned at Eloise. He too had begun as a student and had excelled to a level that Edward Garrett asked him to teach for the studio. He was young but not too young. In his early twenties, he had been a shy teenager who found dancing brought out something in him that he had not had before – confidence. Lee still blushed when he heard something about himself that was complimentary and always walked around with a bit of a lightness in his step and a sparkle in his eye. His wavy brown hair and tall lean body was perfect for a dance teacher. Yes, he was the picture perfect look for one who taught dance. Mary Lou Smith knew he would be one of her most prized assets here in the new studio.

Kenneth Andrews and Becca Fine walked in together chatting about the walls and the desk and the floor and the ceilings. Kenneth had an odd look to him. He had a bright blond hair color and large round black rimmed glasses on a pale white face. Kenneth was a bit doughy in appearance because he seemed so pale – almost albino. Becca was pretty. She had shoulder length dark brown hair that Edward always tried to coax her to add a few streaks to. So far she hadn't listened to him. It was all natural with a bouncy fullness. Although she was lean and muscular, she would always appear heavy when next to Charlotte who was more elfin and delicate boned.

Mary Lou simmered in her office as the waves of laughter drifted out from the teachers' office. The whole group was together and they liked each other. That was almost too much for her to take as she sat alone in her own office – an executive cast-off. She would never feel that she could communicate again with them on a teacher-teacher level. She was forever banished upward, never to come down again. It was lonely up there in the executive office.

They pulled out a small table and some stacking chairs for a brief first meeting of the studio staff. Eloise sat behind the desk peering out carefully with a watchful eye. Old students seem to think something magical will happen during the hours they are not usually there. They wait for the whooping and hollering to happen any moment, and their faces show the disappointment when it never comes. That was the way Eloise Parker was – anxious but disappointed. Every so often during the meeting Mary Lou would bellow "Parker" when she needed a schedule or phone number or just to bellow her name. Eloise's lopsided mouth began to dip into discontent.

"Welcome", Mary Lou began. She looked over the four faces and smiled. This would be a great staff. Lee ever so sweet and innocent would have the women students drooling. She couldn't have a more beautiful staff of women than Becca and Charlotte. They would have the men eating out of their hands. And Kenneth. Well, Kenneth would be the artistic one – the one who would always keep them dancing and perfecting their craft. He would make sure they try the harder steps and put together something interesting when they choreographed their routines. Yes, he would bring out the best in all of them as dancers. She smiled again. This was a money making staff. And the money would make her the top manager in the Midwest. "Now to go over the plans for the Grand Opening…".

IV.

Mary Lou Smith stood at the front door looking elegant in a long black formal gown beaded along the neckline in sparkling gems. She had found the dress on the sale rack of an upscale women's clothing store and had snatched it up immediately knowing the studio would provide just the right setting for something so glamorous. She had tried to smooth out her curly hair and wore a bright red lip shade. Each and every guest to enter was greeted with "I'm Mary Lou Smith, the manager of this beautiful new studio. Welcome!"

Edward Garrett was of course late, but mingling among the guests he had personally invited. He had immediately found Charlotte Papalo when he first arrived greeting her with a lingering hug and kiss on the cheek. She had smiled and after a moment managed to slither quietly into the crowd. Charlotte's soothing beige chiffon gown wrapped several times with a braided gold band didn't stand out well in a crowd because of its subdued color and soft lines. She easily moved to the edge of the floor and began to greet potential students.

Kenneth and Lee wore black tails. Edward told them it was a must and after meeting the many executive men from the large corporations who wore expensive and well tailored tuxes, they were grateful for the advice. They fit in nicely and received rave reviews from the women guests. Becca Fine wore a simple black dress with black dress heels and a choker of pearls around her neck. Soft dance music played in the background. The downtown staff manned the food table serving champagne, cheese and crackers, and fresh fruit. There was a tray of chocolates and a beautiful torte sliced and ready to eat. Usually Edward was very careful not to allow "junky" food when he was on one of his health food kicks, but today was special and even he grabbed a piece of torte.

"I'll have to exercise extra hard tomorrow," he had winked at Suzanna Caldwell as she moved aside so he could snatch the plate. Every morning at exactly 9:15 am, Edward had his exercise class in the downtown studio. Originally it was to teach the staff some new dance moves and keep them in tip top shape, but lately it was because he was feeling old. He would invite other "friends" who didn't teach in the studio to join him. This list usually included some of the top models in the city area. With all the beautiful people staring at him in the mirror each morning, it made him try that much harder to do more leg lifts and more spins and more repetitions. It was easy to see what motivated Edward Garrett the most. Himself.

At the height of the evening, Edward called to the crowd. "Attention everyone! Greetings on this exquisite evening and welcome. I hope you are enjoying the new space, the food, and the music. Hopefully, you are also enjoying the dancing." Several of the teachers had begun to dance a few steps with their students. "I'd like to introduce the staff of this beautiful new studio to you…" . He had the group line up and introduced each one. Mary Lou Smith graced the end of the line. "And to show you just how fabulous you can look out on the dance floor…", he put his hand out to Charlotte and invited her to the center of the room with him. They danced an elegant Waltz, her dress swirling on the turns, and her smile charming all those who had any doubts they might never be able to get out on a floor and move like that. Mary Lou Smith stood in the corner with a plastic smile plastered to her face. She tried to look proud but was beginning to wilt with envy. Then Edward and Charlotte danced a sensuous

Rumba that brought claps from all corners of the room. Once again Edward presented Charlotte and gave her another kiss on the cheek as she smiled sweetly.

"That was uncalled for," Mary Lou muttered under her breath all the while continuing to smile and clap. She would have a few choice words for the great Mr. Edward Garrett once the ballroom cleared out. Eloise Parker stood behind her in a tiny mint green mini skirt and flowered top doing her best to blend into the back wall. She quickly scurried back to her post in the reception area before anyone noticed the desk was unmanned.

The long evening ended abruptly with the entire staff lined up in a final reception line to say a pleasant good night to all guests. As the twenty plus staff hurried to clean up the food, the tables, and the floor, Mary Lou Smith clung to the front desk asking Parker for a final report on sample lessons scheduled. She had carefully explained before the doors opened that evening that appointments were Eloise Parker's key responsibility that evening.

"I am pleased to report that we have scheduled both Miss Papalo and Miss Fine with a full week's schedule. Lee is completely booked as well and Kenneth is about half full at this point," Eloise had reading glasses propped on her round Nordic nose as she carefully avoided eye contact with Miss Smith.

"Wonderful! Did you schedule each of those appointments with a chat session on my schedule?"

"Well, um. Did you want me to put all of these in your schedule also?" Eloise grimaced at the words she was expecting from Miss Smith when she discovered she had not done something correctly.

Instead, Mary Lou said quite pleasantly, "Yes, you can just write in a little time with me after each lesson even if I have to double, triple or quadruple book. I don't care! I'll do anything I have to for this studio to get off to a good start. Just put them all in and I'll manage somehow." Then she walked away from the desk with a quick step and a relaxed hum to the background music that was still playing. Eloise looked relieved and quickly penciled in all of the appointments scheduled that evening into Miss Smith's column on the large scheduling sheet clipped to her desk. More, more and still more. That was what Mary Lou Smith expected, and Eloise would remember that from this day on.

The weekly meeting between the executive staff members from both studios was typically in the downtown studio. Although Mary Lou dreaded that rush hour drive every Friday morning into the city, parking, and then trudging into Edward's dark and stuffy office, she enjoyed the reports she always brought with her. Suzanna was now joined in the executive meetings by Antoine Hawks who just became the counselor of the new student department in the city studio. So the four of them, Mary Lou, Suzanna, Antoine and Edward, would gather to discuss the figures and the issues facing each studio. In spite of the smaller staff, the newness of the suburban studio brought lots of new business and huge numbers. But Mary Lou in spite of giving the appearance of satisfaction with her results during these meetings was never really content. She always wanted more.

Today she carried her black brief case along with a large coffee and paused at the front desk to gaze out on the dance floor. Edward was again finishing up his morning exercise class. There were a number of models she recognized who were constants in this session, but there in the back was a new face. Edward was paying special attention to her as he would pause to show a new move. She was definitely someone Edward would be drawn to – slender and beautiful with long hair streaming behind her. The rest of the group in spite of being models looked a bit shabby in comparison. They had their hair plopped on top of their heads, wore tights with gaping holes and too large sweatshirts over their leos. This new one wore a tiny sparkly pink leo with no tights and no cover up. She had a full face of makeup and as she flung her mane of hair, didn't even seem to sweat from the workout.

As Edward walked off the floor, Mary Lou grabbed his arm. Motioning with a nod of her head she asked, "So who's the new one?"

"Miss Jilli Wilson. My new teacher," he said proudly with a grin as he pulled his knit cap down lower on his head. Edward always exercises minus his toupee so wore a knit hat to hide his quickly balding head.

"I want her," Mary Lou demanded.

"What?" he pulled back with a start.

"I want her in my studio. I have Charlotte and Becca completely booked and I need a new female teacher right now. I'll take her." Mary Lou gazed into his eyes. Whatever she had on Edward Garrett, now scared and startled him once again. His eyes widened, and he pursed his lips before licking them gingerly. "OK. I'll send her out this afternoon after our meeting. But she continues to come to morning exercise. No booking her in the mornings. Understand?"

"Understood." And she did understand. Jilli Wilson was to be his new conquest.

V.

"Miss Smith," Eloise called over the new intercom system. "Pick up for Miss Caldwell on line two."

Mary Lou lifted the phone and heard Suzanna babble on about a Christmas party. Mary Lou was only half listening but managed to hear that the staff Christmas party would be this weekend at Suzanna's apartment. They had a new couple in the city studio that owned one of the prominent jewelry stores in the area, and Edward suggested that she pick out pieces of gold for each staff member as their Christmas gift from him.

"What would you suggest might be nice for your staff?" Suzanna asked.

"Well, I'd say not to worry about sizing things, so a bracelet might be nice for each of them. Of course for me, I wear a size 5 ½ ring," she said hinting at the added cost her gift might have as an executive staff member.

Suzanna chatted a bit more then reminded Mary Lou to give the party information to her staff along with her

26

address. Mary Lou pondered. When so much of the day was dedicated to students and business, it was always a pleasant diversion to get the staff together not about dancing, but just to socialize. This might be just the break she needed from all the pressures to keep up and do better and be the best. She never realized how driven she was and what a toll it took. She felt old. She had hit thirty, and it made her feel like the grandmother of the group. Now with Jilli Wilson added to the staff, she dreaded the staff photo with the three beauties and the little short old person at the end of the row. She would go to the party and have a nice relaxed evening. With the party being held at Suzanna's apartment, there would be no room for dancing. It would just be a social time, and maybe she needed that more than she thought. No skirt, no makeup, and no sore feet.

Jilli Wilson had been a blessing to the suburban studio. She didn't have the dance experience that the other staff members had, but she had a naïve beauty that attracted her not only to the other staff members but to the students. They really didn't care if she was a fabulous dancer yet or not. Just to put their arms around her in a dance position and stare into her lovely eyes was enough. Where Charlotte was a beauty with brains, Jilli was a beauty with a heart.

"So tell me, Jilli," Mary Lou had said to her one week as she waited for the executive meeting downtown. "Why do you wear a skimpy leotard when all the others exercising wear all those leg warmers and tights and things to keep them warm in this chilly studio?"

Jilli had looked around with a confused look in her eyes as if seeing for the first time that she was indeed the only one dressed so lightly. "Well, Mr. Garrett told me when I first came in to exercise that he required I wear only a leotard, so that is what I do."

"Doesn't it seem odd that no one else seems to have that restriction?" Mary Lou hoped she was giving her enough of a hint to see clearly Edward's true intentions with that request. She hoped Jilli would recognize that Edward was just a dirty old man who had an agenda that wasn't quite so honorable.

Jilli looked around again and blinking a bit didn't say another word. But Mary Lou noticed that she went to her bag to pull on a sweater over the leo just a few moments later.

Jilli and Lee Watkins seemed to enjoy dancing together during the staff dance sessions. As quiet and shy as Lee was, he seemed to blush the entire dance session when paired with Jilli. Jilli didn't mind – or didn't really notice and began to really improve in her dance skills with all the added practice they were doing before the start of the day and at the end after lessons were over. It seemed an unlikely match, but who knew what would or could happen. Nothing is ever as it seems.

The staff Christmas party was a soothing and enjoyable event in the midst of a busy season in both the studios and in everyone's private lives. They all sat around on the big overstuffed couch and on the floor munching on snacks and watching Edward Garrett's old home movies. Edward enjoyed taking pictures and filming almost as much as he enjoyed collecting music – a passion that served the studio well in light of the nature of the business. Edward's music collection was amazing. He always wanted to play a new piece of music he had found and experiment with new dance moves to go with it. That was the beauty of his choreography – it was new and innovative because of his interest in current music trends. He was ahead of the game.

He flipped on his old home movie of studio functions and got to a clip of some dancers up on the stage in bright red hot pants and hats that were popular during the early 70's.

Suzanna yelped with excitement. "This is one of the first hustle routines you will ever see. Edward choreographed this for a New York dance convention and the crowd went wild. They had never seen anything like it before."

They all watched intently the unique moves danced by the three couples on the stage. It went by too quickly and they asked to rewind again and again. Newer teachers were thrilled with the stage and the costumes and the whole setting of the routine.

"So who are these people?" Jilli Wilson piped up moving closer to the screen.

"What?" Suzanna giggled. "That's me and Dennis Whit on the left, Edward is with Elenor Reece – no longer with the studio, and there's Mary Lou on the right with Mr. Collin, another former teacher."

"Wow," Jilli gasped. "Mary Lou you are so very tiny and such a great dancer."

The entire staff pulled their gaze from the screen and stared at Mary Lou. It was very believable to see Suzanna up there. Her glasses and same styled hair made her stand out. She was a bit thinner and younger back then. But Mary Lou Smith wasn't even recognizable. She looked like a little girl – tiny, frail, and a whip of a spinner.

"Rhythm dances were always my forte and Suzanna was the smooth one." Mary Lou nodded as she chomped into a piece of pizza. "But too many pieces of this stuff will give you this." And she stood to let them view her older and wider body.

They watched the film a few more times, eventually asking Edward if they could do a revival of the number he had choreographed. "Actually this stuff is going to get very hot in just a few weeks time. This song we used is coming back on a movie soundtrack and should be an even bigger hit the second time around. So, yes this would be a great number to do again. You all want to learn it?"

They all nodded and then headed to the food table for a bit more nourishment before exchanging gifts. Some had small little packages for favorite partners or gag gifts for other staff members that made everyone howl in laughter, but the highlight was the gifts Edward Garrett handed out personally. Of course Suzanna had done all of the actual shopping, but he was given credit for pairing just the right piece of jewelry to the right person. Each took their tiny black box tied with a gold ribbon and oohed and aahed at the glittering gold inside. Most of the women received bracelets and the men received either a heavy bracelet or a chain. When Edward finally passed the gift box to Mary Lou, it was odd shaped. Not the long and narrow bracelet box nor the flat square box of the necklace. Instead it was tiny. Yes, it was a ring with her birthstone inside. It was beautiful and very expensive. She hid in the back corner as she unwrapped so no one else would see exactly what it was or how much it was worth. She slid next to Suzanna and gave her a hug. "Thanks," she whispered into Suzanna's ear. "I know it was you who picked this out, and it's perfect." Then she went up to Edward to thank him and show him how perfect it looked on her finger. It was the end of a really great party. A beautiful gift – not only the ring but the respect that Mary Lou suddenly received from her staff after viewing the routine tape of her dancing. They suddenly looked and saw a new person in front of them.

The next few days were amazing for Mary Lou Smith. Staff members would come up to her asking her to help them with a dance step or asking advice about an amalgamation they were working out for a student. She suddenly was overwhelmed with the added attention her dance expertise was bringing. So it was no small wonder that when the staff dance session, usually taught by Charlotte, decided upon a staff routine for the upcoming

Festival party, they included Mary Lou as an important part of their formation.

Festival was a magical time of year. The new suburb studio was already busy with new students. With only five teachers on staff who were teaching lessons, their schedules were already booked solid, but the opportunities that the Festival brought were enormous. Festival was held yearly for a six week period to build up the student count in most studios. There was always a theme for the series of parties held during those weeks. But unlike the weekly practice parties that they always had, these parties were special. They had decorations and costumes and exciting routines and food. It was a time that really built up the benefits of learning to dance for the current students and allowed new students to participate in all of the festivities and get excited about what they were experiencing.

This year the parties would be special because the two studios would hold the parties together. They would alternate studios allowing the students and staff from each studio to see and host the other one. The theme was "Broadway" and each party took a Broadway play or musical to portray. "The Phantom of the Opera" would be elegant and sophisticated with lots of Waltz , Viennese Waltz, and beautiful flowing gowns. "42nd Street" would feature the swing and fox trots popular during the 1930's and 40's. There would be hot music and zoot suits. "Oklahoma" would be a cowboy and country western theme. Everyone would get out their boots and Stetson hats for a rousing good time at the two step and cotton eyed Joe. But the most anticipated and exciting party was to be the "West Side Story" party to take place at the new suburb studio. The large back ballroom would be transformed into a New York street scene complete with the two rival gangs competing in a dance-off. The suburb studio would be the Latin Sharks and the Downtown gang would portray the rival Jets.

Charlotte had spent hours listening to the music from "West Side Story" and knew the song "America" would be the Mambo they must dance. The Latin Mambo was one hot dance. Fast and furious with lots of hip motion and spins, she carefully chose the patterns they would use. Normally, their staff routine would consist of two couples dancing – they only had two male dancers. The women would switch off dancing. But this time, Charlotte was determined to include everyone and that meant asking Mary Lou to dance with them. Four women and two men in a fast Mambo with quick feet action and a unique formation that would begin with a line that moved into different challenge pieces.

Mary Lou didn't say so, but Charlotte could tell she was honored and excited to finally show off her dance skills to the students who saw her as the old lady who hovered occasionally but usually spent her days holed up in her office with paperwork. They would receive the shock of their lives. Mary Lou would be the center of the routine.

When the party night finally arrived, the downtown staff wandered in an hour or so before the party was to start. They had been teaching all day and carpooled out to the new studio at the very last possible moment carrying garment bags of costumes and an excited anticipation of going head to head with the "new" staff.

The moment of the dance-off finally came and the Jets dressed in jeans, white t-shirts and slicked back hair stormed the dance floor. The students in their own unique costumes spread out around the edges of the floor leaving the space in the middle open for the anticipated dance. "We are the Jets..." began to play over the music system and they were off, dancing a lively jive. Of course, the students from the downtown studio clapped the loudest as they stood solidly behind their own studio staff. Suzanna stood at the music system watching with pride as her teachers did some fun lifts and fast footwork. Edward Garrett was manning the sound system as usual. He always attended the Festival parties and tried to bring his famous music collection in for the enjoyment of the students and staff. Of course, sometimes his taste in music brought some unfavorable comments from students who "couldn't find the beat".

Edward's face showed the enjoyment he received from this lively exchange. He nodded approvingly as the Jets showed their best stuff out on the floor. But just as quickly, the tide changed. Next it was the Shark's turn. The six teachers snaked out to the floor wearing tight black pants and t-shirts accented with hot pink and red scarves wrapped around their necks and waists. Lining up, Mary Lou Smith was positioned right in the middle with the taller women to each side of her and the two men mixed in. The "America" song began and they danced quickly forward from the back of the ballroom with a series of quick flicks and turns. The crowd picked up the spirit of the Mambo and hooted their approval. This time it wasn't only the suburb students cheering but the downtown students as well. It was a great routine that cleverly showed the fast hips and feet of the dancers. When they finished, it was clear from the applause that the "new" gang had won.

Edward invited the students and other staff members to join in and dance the Mambo – the floor was mobbed with dancers eager to try out their moves.

Mary Lou Smith panted with exhaustion and headed for the punch bowl where she was met with a pat on the back from Edward Garrett who was also grabbing a glass of punch. "Nice job," he nodded. That was about the best compliment anyone could expect from him. But it meant a lot, just those few words.

As the party began to wind down, the staff stood in their ritual receiving line to say a farewell to the students and guests then on to cleaning up the studio. Suzanna Caldwell looked around as if trying to decide what to do first. She twisted her mouth into a tight purse and turned to Eloise Parker at the front desk. "Have you by chance spotted Edward Garrett?" she asked scanning the dance floor.

Eloise was finishing up a phone call and shook her head. Suzanna spotted Charlotte laughing with one of her staff members and Jilli Wilson was helping Lee carry the food table now cleared to the back hallway for storage. Kenneth was bragging about their routine a bit to one of the downtown staffers as they both swept down the floor. Mary Lou was no where to be seen. She let out a puff of frustrated air and turned to knock on Edward's door. The light was visibly on underneath the door but there was no answer from within so she turned the knob hoping not to catch him in a compromising position which was always possible with Edward. Instead to her horror she spotted Edward slumped in his chair, head cocked to the side with a wide eyed gaze in his eyes. Quickly she ran in hoping to find a pulse.

"Call 911!" she screamed frantically. "Call 911!"

By the time the paramedics arrived, Edward Garrett was dead.

There was nothing unusual in Edward's office – nothing out of place. Everyone assumed that even at his young age, he must have had a heart attack. But that was not the case. They would find out soon enough that Edward Garrett was indeed murdered. Poison they said. Something in his punch. After interviewing a few of the party guests and staff, the police took Mary Lou Smith down to the police station. Enough people had reported the two of them standing together at the punch bowl earlier to warrant a more detailed interview with Miss Smith. Charlotte stood by the desk with Becca and Jilli as they escorted her out the door. Clearly their faces showed the horror of the evening. First a death, now ruled a murder and then the possible accusation of their own leader and friend. A chill ran through the room and the stillness was frightening.

VI.

When Mary Lou was released from the police station, she immediately called Suzanna. They agreed to meet for lunch at an out of the way Italian restaurant downtown. Sliding into a back booth for privacy, Mary Lou talked briefly about her police station experience.

"The only story that kept popping up was my standing next to Edward at the punch table after our dance off. They have no evidence at all to suggest that I had anything to do with Edward's death," she summed up the events coolly they broke down a bit. "But Suzanna," she pleaded suddenly, "you have to help me because if they don't find the real killer, I will always be the prime suspect. I'll always look guilty of this terrible thing. And I didn't do anything, I swear."

Suzanna nodded. In spite of their years of rivalry, she couldn't believe that Mary Lou would suddenly kill Edward Garrett. There had been so many rough times between the two of them in the past that would have certainly prompted murder if she had actually decided to get rid of the man. Now was a good time, a productive time, a time of plenty for both of them. It certainly would not have been advantageous for Mary Lou to commit such a crime at this time.

Their food came to the table and Suzanna carefully folded her white cloth napkin across her lap as she stared intently at the plate of steaming pasta in front of her. It looked good. Mary Lou hardly noticed her plate.

Mary Lou continued on. "It had to be another of the staff. But who?"

"Why not a student?" Suzanna suggested sipping her hot tea and picking up her fork for a first bite.

"Now why would you say that? A student? Why would a student have anything against Edward Garrett?"

"I can think of a number of reasons. Someone may think Edward sets his price for lessons too high. They might think he is draining their savings. A relative might worry that a mother or father or grandparent is spending their inheritance on frivolous dance lessons. Edward could have spurned someone who was interested in him romantically. Now that one isn't too much of a stretch to imagine." Suzanna started to rattle off reasons and

40

probably could have gone on indefinitely but had made her point quite clearly. She sat back and peered over her glasses.

"I hadn't thought of those reasons," Mary Lou frowned. "That makes it even harder because now there is a whole room full of suspects. How many would you say attended that party?"

Suzanna laughed and shook her head. "Let's put our heads together and keep our eyes and ears open for anything unusual. There must be someone out there who was particularly angry at Edward. We need to be very aware of everything and everyone around us." The plan was agreed upon by both. Once rivals, now they were partners in their determination to solve this crime. Then they enjoyed their meals with the added satisfaction that their friendship might help them find a killer.

At the daily meeting in the suburb studio Charlotte raised her hand. "I have a suggestion," she began when Mary Lou gave her a quick nod of the head. "I think we should revive Mr. Garrett's hustle routine. As a sort of tribute to him and his memory. Both studios could work together to reconstruct that very routine. I think he would be honored if we could perform his choreography."

The others nodded in agreement and even Mary Lou thought the idea was a worthwhile suggestion. She actually felt very excited about doing that very routine again. It brought back special memories of a time in her life when she loved and cherished her own dancing. She would call Suzanna and make the suggestion so each studio could begin work on the amalgamations. Charlotte thought Mary Lou could teach her staff the routine and Suzanna could do the same for the downtown staff.

Suzanna was actually thrilled with the idea. Not only was it a great tribute to Edward, but it gave the staff a project during this time of sorrow and confusion.

Mary Lou met Suzanna at her apartment to view the tape again and remember long forgotten moves. Watching again and again, they reminisced about the early days when the downtown studio first opened. Times had certainly changed. First, Edward no longer had his hair. That fact made them laugh as they recalled how he had reacted as his hair slowly began to thin. When he had reluctantly purchased his first toupee, it had been a day both remembered clearly.

"I remember him walking into the studio with that first rug," Suzanna recalled. "He was so tense that no one said anything at all in case it might set him off on one of his temper tantrums. So we all just sat there quietly staring as he began the meeting. Remember?"

"Do I? Of course. We were all so timid back then. He was such a powerful force in the studio. No one wanted to make him angry. He didn't control his temper back then as much as he does today – er, as much as he did. I can't really imagine him dead and not around. It all seems like a bad dream that will suddenly be over with him back smiling his loopy smile and tapping his feet nervously. I'll miss that hideous sound – his tap tap tapping."

The moment became solemn. They both didn't say anything for a short time and just kept their eyes on the film. After a discussion of the moves and sequence of the steps, they wrote down notes to bring back to their respective studios. It was not an easy routine to do with the quick footwork and large swinging arm movements. It was truly a brilliant piece of choreography.

"OK let's go over this introduction," Mary Lou was telling her staff the next day at the dance session. Quickly she began to show the dancers the basic movement of the rope hustle and the position of the couple to each other. "Notice the arm movements used by the men in leading this pattern," she explained. "This arm motion is not easy but it's what makes the appearance of this dance so showy – big and noticeable."

She carefully showed the women a low lunge that was in the middle of the dance. "You'll want to start practicing this movement right away or else your legs won't be strong enough to get the next part – the hip up. It takes a lot of strength to do this and I will warn you, you will be sore tomorrow." They all began practicing the lunge and indeed it did take a toll on each of them as both Becca and Jilli stiffly began to shake out their lead legs to relieve the pain.

"Wow, this is tough," Jilli complained. But immediately she tried another one with a grimace.

The routine brought the staff together as each day they learned more and more of the patterns. The harder movements began to look better and feel better. There was also a change in the atmosphere at the studio. There was romance in the air.

First, Charlotte came in with a new lightness in her step. "I've found me a new man," she announced in her sweet breathy voice one morning as she checked her messages at the front desk.

"Details," Mary Lou begged as she rummaged through the stack of appointment sheets for the day.

"Too early to talk about," she said with a sly twinkle in her eye.

Then that afternoon Becca received a beautiful bouquet of red roses – at least two dozen large red roses. She too wouldn't say anything but looked pleased as she carried the vase back to her desk in the teachers' office.

Lee and Jilli Wilson often times left together at the end of the studio day. Now they were starting to come into the studio together as well. "An odd couple," Mary Lou thought as she watched the shy Lee gaze fondly after the Bambish Jilli. Jilli didn't seem to notice the affect she had on Lee. She didn't notice him stammering when he spoke to her and didn't notice the blushes when she teased him.

Mary Lou couldn't help but wonder as she watched her staff if any of them had anything to do with Edward Garrett's murder. Surely, Charlotte had been a favorite of Edward's. He was always paying close attention to her. Always giving her a quick kiss on the cheek and a hug whenever he could get close to her. She didn't seem to notice, or if she did notice, she shunned his advances gracefully without causing him to feel rejected. Charlotte was very good at soothing the boiling pot of water. There was an art to her reactions.

Jilli on the other hand was also clearly a favorite, but she didn't seem to notice at all. Maybe Edward reacted to her the same way all men reacted to her. Maybe it was so normal for men to fawn and drool over her beauty that she just thought it to be quite normal. Her students were the same way. They all just stared and gawked and glowed in her presence. It was rather disturbing for any woman who wasn't Jilli Wilson to watch the reaction of all of these men. It would seem that if anyone were jealous, they would have poisoned Jilli Wilson instead of Edward Garrett.

But perhaps the most surprising romance of all involved Eloise Parker. It was one day just before the daily meeting when Eloise seated behind the large desk became quite excited. Staring out into the hallway, she quickly motioned the man standing in the doorway to come in. She stood to peer over the top of the desk and smiled. Then reaching over the desk she gave the man a quick peck on the cheek and they whispered heads together for a time before Mary Lou who was watching from her office ambled out to the desk to see what was happening. As she neared the reception area, she notice the man was actually very young – no more than perhaps twenty years old. He had slightly thinning hair and glasses which made him appear middle aged from a distance. He appeared to be shorter than Eloise who was not a very tall person herself. Mary Lou could only think of the TV dough boy when she looked at him. He was not heavy, but rather round and well, soft looking.

"Miss Smith, this is Ben my new boyfriend," Eloise gushed as she introduced the two.

Ben turned with a grin and stuck out his hand for a shake. Mary Lou was a bit slow but did take his extended hand and shook. The surprise was that Eloise was definitely over forty years old although she did want desperately to be young. That clearly showed in the way she dressed. Eloise was always wearing something short, tight and fashionable to the younger teen set. If the new style was to wear a top a couple inches above your natural waistline, well, Eloise would have one on. If the new trend was a short skirt, then Eloise would wear one that barely covered. Often times Mary Lou thought Eloise must be stuck too long behind the desk and never ventured out to actually view herself in the long floor to ceiling mirrors that graced the ballroom walls. She couldn't possibly think she was dressed in a flattering way, was the thought that almost daily popped into Mary Lou's mind as she watched Eloise strut through the reception area. Now this Ben was another attempt at looking and feeling young. Yet as she talked with him, she couldn't help but think how perfect this man was for Eloise Parker. Somehow they seemed in spite of the age difference to be made for each other. It was really a head shaking wonder. She was sure they would be seeing this Ben frequently, and she was right. Ben would pop in on his lunch hour every day to chit chat with Eloise.

Miss Martin was a young student of about twenty eight or twenty nine. That was actually very young for the suburb studio who seemed to attract older and more established couples or middle aged men and women feeling the effects of a divorce. Miss Martin, one of Lee's students, on the other hand was a short energetic woman who was on her way to becoming quite a good dancer. She had her hair short with a bit of a wave and was constantly on some sort of faddish diet. Her round glasses were always removed for a competition or performance to reveal a heavy coating of shadow and liner. She always seemed naked without those glasses perched on her nose.

Today she bounced into the studio early. Mary Lou watched her from her office as she propped her box on a table in the small dance studio and threw down a shoe bag. Without so much as an acknowledgement to anyone she proceeded to pull out scissors and a stapler along with stacks of brightly colored paper from her box. Eloise was so far hidden behind the desk that she didn't seem to notice Miss Martin at all and the music playing muffled any sounds that the cutting would make. Cutting and snipping what appeared to be hot pink and yellow fringes, Miss Martin began to shimmy and shake to the music that was playing. Then she began her stapling with big whomps on the cork board that hung by the small stereo sound system next to the desk.

Mary Lou finally was so curious that she got up, pushed her reading glasses back up her nose and walked across the ballroom in her squeaky sensible shoes. She stood behind Miss Martin and watched as she began pinning up colorful pictures.

"Oh, I didn't see you!" Miss Martin looked truly surprised as she did a quick Samba turn and came face to face with Mary Lou standing with her hands on her hips. "Pictures from the Festival. I took so many that I thought the other students – and staff – might like to see all of the highlights from the parties." She handed a picture to Mary Lou of the dance off with Mary Lou right in the middle hunched in a position to lead the "Sharks" to victory. Mary Lou picked up a stack and thumbed through them. They were very nice – well centered and capturing some great expressions. There was one of the Sharks and another of the Jets. Some of Edward Garrett standing at the microphone playing the party music.

Mary Lou sucked in a breath. It was difficult to see a picture of Edward. Difficult and yet it made her smile to see him happily pounding on his bongos as he always did during the Festival parties with his wide mouthed grin.

Miss Martin had put a colorful background on the board and explained the fringe was actually supposed to be curtains to represent the Broadway Musical theme they had for the parties. It was a nice gesture and Mary Lou thanked her before she squeaked across the floor back to her office.

VII.

Anna Smith was a teacher in the downtown studio. She was the best advanced teacher they had because of her experience – she had been teaching for about three years – and because of her beautiful dance technique. Anna was only about nineteen years old but appeared to be older. She was not a person you would imagine could be a dancer with her stocky body and tightly curled short matronly hair. But when she stepped on the dance floor no one could keep their eyes off of her. Her balance and impeccable movement was breathtaking. Not only was she one of

Mary Lou's favorite dancers, but she was also Mary Lou's younger sister although one would never guess from her appearance. Mary Lou was short and compact; Anna was taller and rather large boned. They looked to be from completely different worlds and yet they were from the same one.

Mary Lou loved to get together with Anna and find out all of the downtown gossip. She had originally wanted Anna to be a part of her staff out in the suburb studio, but Edward would not even consider that possibility. He was probably right. It was better for both of them to be apart and not together every day. Maybe then they would not have the great relationship they had always been able to share as sisters. This Saturday morning, Mary Lou had invited Anna to join her for a brunch at her small apartment. She was anxious to share with her the police station ordeal and get some perspective from Anna about Edward's untimely death. They hadn't spoken at any great length since the Mambo party about the murder.

Mary Lou set out some Danish and fruit along with a carafe of coffee on her small kitchen table. She had a tiny breakfast nook surrounded by windows between the kitchen and the living room in her efficiency apartment. It was surprisingly cozy and an area she enjoyed that kept her mind off of studio and studio problems. She gazed across the kitchen counter to the bright stillness created by the sunlight shining in through the windows and catching the array of knick knacks she had scattered on the corner shelves. The small pieces had been the only items she took from her mother's house when she died. They reminded her of her childhood and the great love her mother had shown in raising her three children. Their father had left the family when Mary Lou was young, and she didn't know if he was alive or dead. He hadn't shown up for her mother's funeral and for all she knew he could be in prison or drunk on the streets. That seemed to be the pattern he had chosen for his life before he abandoned them. But her mother had strength – just like Mary Lou had to make the best of her life.

Anna showed up with her usual bundle of energy and swooned with delight at the stack of Danish. Edward had always hounded her to lose weight, but she never paid much attention to Edward's rants. She was secure with herself and her image of herself. His constant nagging only made her laugh.

Mary Lou proceeded to tell Anna about her visit to the police station. "I'm about the best suspect they have because apparently I'm the one everyone saw standing with him at the punch bowl. And Edward's punch cup was spiked with some type of poison." Mary Lou tried to seem nonchalant but her voice showed a slight waver as she spoke.

"Ridiculous!" Anna ranted. "I heard rumors in the downtown studio that they were checking into Edward committing suicide."

Mary Lou frowned. "That just doesn't seem possible." Mary Lou thought about that night and recalled how energetic and excited Edward was during the party. Of course, he always seemed that way when there were people around and a party going on. She had known Edward for so long that she knew when he was alone he worried about getting old, getting out of shape, getting bald and just about everything else. She knew that his energy was a wall masking his fear. She knew he didn't sleep well at night. On many a dance trip she had seen him down a bottle of cold medicine to help him sleep at night. But suicide? It didn't seem possible to her. Could he have taken something by accident?

Anna continued. "I don't know how that could be. He was in his new religious kick and seemed to be in a constant state of 'Praise the Lord' and good will lately."

When Mary Lou looked puzzled by this last statement, Anna went on to explain. "You know how Edward never does anything half way. He goes into something 150% even if it's destructive."

Mary Lou nodded. "When he drinks, he's a knock down drunk. When he's into drugs, he wears the coke spoon around his neck. When he's into women, he runs around with anyone on legs. And when he's on a diet he has everyone else in the studio eating whatever his new menu dictates."

Anna laughed. "Remember when we had the head judge from the National Dance Board visiting and in the middle of dance session we took a break for lunch. Edward had a table set up with seeds and nuts. The judge made the comment about feeling like a bird." The two of them laughed until tears rolled down their faces as they recalled the incident.

"Well," Anna continued when they had stopped. "Edward got involved with that Pentecostal church a couple of blocks from the downtown area and he's been – or was – getting very involved. He was talking about religion and being saved and all kinds of things lately."

"How did I not notice that?" Mary Lou muttered.

"You are out in the suburb studio and away from the every day things that went on with Edward," Anna reminded her.

It was true. Edward never came out to the studio in the suburbs. He had intended to, but never quite made it. They were pretty much isolated from the day to day things Mary Lou had experienced when in the downtown studio. Edward never called. He just took her weekly report every Friday in their short meeting and sent her on her way. Because the studio was new and attracting all kinds of suburb students that refused to venture downtown, he had pretty much left her and her staff alone.

Mary Lou began to formulate a new plan. She and Suzanna had agreed to keep their eyes and ears opened for information regarding Edward's death, but maybe Mary Lou should make a visit to this church that Edward was frequenting to see if there might be a connection. It was worth the trip. "Where did you say this church was?"

VIII.

The romance in the studio was so thick that Mary Lou found herself gauging whenever she heard Eloise refer to the "dough boy" as "Benjy" – her new pet name. It was almost too much. Lee and Jilli were definitely a couple. She had to have a chat with them about not showing their affection toward each other in front of students and maintaining a professional appearance at all times. Then there was Becca.

Becca received another enormous and expensive bouquet of exotic flowers. Now she had two vases of overpowering flower bunches on her desk that were beginning to brown. Charlotte, ever the motherly figure in the group, had carefully taken the first bouquet to the trash can while cleaning out the beautifully cut vase and returning it to an appropriate place in Becca's cupboard. Charlotte also began to take off the dead leaves from the second bouquet so bits of debris weren't scattering all over the floor and countertops.

Becca with her smoldering brown eyes and thick dark hair didn't seem to notice any of the mess the flowers were bringing, and surprisingly didn't seem excited or happy about the bouquets after the initial surprise. She also didn't receive any more flowers. That made everyone wonder who this mystery man was and why he had stopped sending gifts. Obviously the flowers he had sent were meant to say something to someone. But what was that? Becca sort of floated through her days with a blank look on her face most of the time. Was this a symptom of love or of something else? She wouldn't say.

Charlotte on the other hand was as cheerful as could be. She hummed and sang as she prepared her dance programs. Charlotte kept an impeccably clean desk. Squarely in the middle was a photo of her large family framed in silver. She was a middle child of nine girls, and all were was beautiful as she was. Now that all were older teens or young adults, they seemed even closer than most families, always phoning each other and getting together on weekends. Charlotte's new relationship soon became another part of the studio romance puzzle. No one knew who the man was until one evening as everyone was preparing to leave an older attractive man with a graying neatly trimmed beard walked in and greeted her with an embrace.

The students were long gone and the rest of the staff was quickly running through the hustle routine at the end of the day. The man simply stood at the front desk with a knowing smile on his face and accepted the quick hug.

"Well?" Mary Lou asked staring at Charlotte and her glowing face. "Aren't you going to introduce all of us?"

With that Charlotte turned a bit pink and went around the group introducing everyone to James in her sweet breathy voice. He looked to be well off, wearing expensive casual clothes and speaking with a slight accent. Mary Lou followed them out to the parking lot where James unlocked a new bright yellow Porsche. That was when Mary Lou noticed that Charlotte had no vehicle in the lot. James must have dropped her off this morning. Maybe he had been out there all the time, every day and she simply hadn't noticed.

The first thing Mary Lou did the next morning was rather tacky. When Charlotte waltzed in, Mary Lou was standing at the desk waiting. "Is he married?" she questioned.

Charlotte wasn't surprised, but she didn't laugh at the question either. "Just because he's older, you think he must be married. Well, he's not. And he's not divorced either. He's just never married." Then she turned away, but just for a second. Turning back she added, "And he's not gay either."

And that was that. Pieces of the puzzle were slowly coming together. But the pieces didn't make it any easier to figure out the picture in the middle.

XI.

Suzanna's call was lengthier than usual. She outlined the memorial service that would be held the next week for Edward at a church in the downtown area. "Edward's children will be flying in to attended," she continued.

Edward had been married to his high school sweetheart but that had ended long ago. His two children from that marriage were always displayed prominently in a small framed photo in the center of his desk at the downtown studio. He hadn't had time to properly array his desk at the suburb studio with personal items otherwise there would certainly have been one there as well. The two children, a girl and a boy, were toddlers smiling at the camera with chubby cheeks and glistening wide eyes. His daughter was dressed in a frilly pink dress and wore the popular patent leather white Mary Jane's. Her curled hair had several tiny pink bows tying up bits of curl. His son was younger and in a tiny dress shirt and bow tie. Edward often spoke of his children with such affection but never seemed to visit them or call them. They had moved to California years before with his ex-wife. How many years would that be now? How old could they be?

Suzanna continued, "They are Edward's heirs so inherit the studios. We'll have to see what they want to do with them. Certainly they have no ties to this part of the country so I can't imagine they want to move here and start managing them. Maybe and hopefully they will see them as an investment and let us do our job as managers."

Oh, my. Suddenly their jobs and their lives in the dance business were on the line. Mary Lou hadn't considered what Edward's death meant to the running of the studios. They could all be out of jobs. The studios could be closed down. Her mind began to tick furiously.

"Suzanna, maybe they will let us buy the studios. Do you have any money?" Mary Lou asked.

"None. And you?"

"Nothing saved. How can you save any money on what we make? I'm beginning to worry. What can we do?" Mary Lou felt a quiver in her voice.

"Let's not think about this situation now until we find out the facts. Let's wait and talk to Casey and Clive when they come." Suzanna was always so sensible.

"Casey and Clive? I had forgotten their names. I guess you are right. So after the Memorial Service is over we will do our tribute to Edward?" Mary Lou had to get past the unknown and focus on the rest of the memorial.

"Yes. That's when we will do our hustle routine. We'll have the tribute party here in the downtown studio because it's closer to the church and will certainly be more convenient to those out of town guests. But we need to get the two staffs together to rehearse a few times before."

Mary Lou and Suzanna discussed possible dates and times for rehearsal. They talked about details such as food and decorations. Suzanna had collected some photos of Edward that would be displayed on a table. She mentioned the possibility of wearing the Cally designer costumes that Edward had invested in during one of his trips to New York. They were glossy lycra leotards with matching skirts in a variety of colors. Each one was unique in the twist of the fabric and the cut of the skirt.

"Those things are so uncomfortable," Mary Lou moaned. She remembered how long the skirts seemed for a short person like herself. It made stepping much less dancing awkward and dangerous as a heel could get caught in the hem or snagged in the looping bottom that often dragged on the floor if the dancer was less than six feet tall. Edward always planned – or hoped - for tall dancers. She had to agree they were lovely to look at and very stylish. There were also enough in the closet for the entire staff so they wouldn't have to invest in something new to wear.

"Ok, I'll agree to those hideous dresses if I can wear the royal blue one. It's the only one that fits me in the front."

Suzanna laughed. "Done!" Then Suzanna added, "I forgot to tell you the police called with an update on Edward's murder."

Mary Lou sat up a bit to listen more carefully. She felt her teeth bite into her lower lip.

"The poison that killed Edward was a combination of several prescription medications. They appear to be unrelated medications for several different conditions which is odd. It seems to indicate they were not prescribed for the same person but for different people, and the combination is what caused his death. The police are once again interviewing everyone who was at the party and checking everyone's prescription history to see who might have had access to any of these medications." Suzanna cleared her throat.

"I heard that some think he committed suicide. Does that fit with these findings?" Mary Lou asked hoping it would take her off the hook as a suspect.

"This evidence doesn't seem to indicate suicide. Of course they didn't actually say that to me. But we'll have to see who these medications implicate. Who knows, maybe Edward was taking some medicine. I don't know of any, do you? I can't recall that he had any conditions that he would need a prescription for." Suzanna realized how little they actually knew about Edward and what he did in his hours away from the studio. It seemed they knew him all too well, then something would come up that left such holes in his life. Even his children coming into town made her realize how ignorant she was about Edward's life. Everything she knew seemed so surface at this moment.

Mary Lou sat in her office with the door closed. Usually she liked to have the door opened so she could view the front desk and the small ballroom. It made her feel she had a finger on all that was happening. Today she wanted to be alone and think about the possibility of life without her dancing and the studio. Not only did this death put her in the hot seat as a suspect, but it put her career and the life she knew for the past few years on the line as well. Who were these two children and what would they want to do with the legacy Edward had left for them? She couldn't recall much if anything about Edward's ex-wife other than the two had known each other growing up. The ex didn't share Edward's dreams of rebuilding the dance business and its reputation in Minneapolis. That had been who he was, but not what she had wanted. Of course, Mary Lou imagined life with Edward had been tough. He was so intense and so focused on what he was doing. She recalled Anna telling her about his recent religious conversion. She would most certainly have to visit this church before the memorial service to get an impression about Edward's new found interest. She would have to meet some of the people and see what their connection with Edward could be. He was such a complicated person.

Sunday morning was quiet. Mary Lou made a point to get to the church well before the service was to begin. She wanted to formulate an opinion by watching and observing those coming into the service as well as peek around the building a bit to see what it was all about. It seemed normal enough. Mary Lou's family had grown up in the Catholic Church, and it hadn't really been much more personally than a bit of gibberish to her. The rules and the kneeling and the Latin mass were all too much for her to comprehend as a child. As soon as she moved out of her mother's house, she had stopped attending services. She realized that was all she knew about church and religion.

The building was large and very well kept. The sanctuary was round and circular with rows and rows of pews centering around a beautiful raised stage and hanging cross. There was no traditional lectern in the front so she was curious where the priest would stand. The high ceilings were lined with vaulted windows and sunlight that gave the whole room a glow. It was truly peaceful. And peaceful was what she needed at that moment. She hadn't realized what a toll the past few days had taken on her physical body and seated in the center of the empty room suddenly relaxed her body. The warm sunlight felt soothing, and the quiet made her eyelids heavy. It was a few moments before anyone else entered.

As the people began to come into the sanctuary they greeted each other and her as well. There were smiles and "Praise God's" and a background music playing that made her feel comfortable. It was so unusual to be nurtured when she was in a people service business that required her to do the greeting and the servicing. People came up and shook her hand and gave hugs to friends. Their faces didn't register. She didn't know who any of these people were, but as the sanctuary filled with people of all ages she felt as if she were in a dream – a cloud so to speak. There was humming and swaying. The music began and she didn't join in the singing but found after a few bars that she too was swaying to the beat. Some of the people were raising their hands toward the ceiling with eyes closed. "Praise the Lord for he is good" resounded from the corners of the room. At times she wanted to turn around and run out of that place. What was happening here?

The pastor stood in the front with a microphone and began to speak – not in Latin as she had remembered from childhood, but in an excited and enthusiastic tone. He didn't talk about sin and condemnation and the evil in the world. Instead he spoke about love and forgiveness and peace. People began to call out "Amen" and clap when he said something profound. She found herself drawn into the spirit of what he was saying. Deep down inside of her, it was comforting to feel a sense that God was with her and guiding her especially since she had felt so alone since she had opened the new studio. She felt overwhelmed with relief. Her eyes followed him as he walked around the raised stage. It felt as if he was personally interacting with each person there.

When the pastor prayed, she felt tears welling up in her eyes. She felt as if she were about to burst. It was such a strange feeling for Mary Lou who was always in control of her emotions. All of the anger and frustration seemed to pour out of her. When the pastor asked those who wanted to accept Jesus as their Savior to come down to the front of the church, she found herself rising out of her seat and walking down the aisle with the others who were migrating toward his voice. It was so powerful.

The whole experience was exhilarating and confusing at the same time. This was not what she had expected at all. Was this what Edward had felt? A sense of relief and peace? She imagined it was. Mary Lou walked the few blocks toward the studio and began to ponder what Edward must have felt the last few weeks of his life. He had died in a good state she reasoned. His mind and his soul had been in a state of calm maybe for the first time in his life. She knew he had lived a life most would not be proud to have lived. He had done many things that she didn't want to know about. But in his final weeks he had felt forgiven and was at peace.

As she entered the studio for rehearsal, she remained in a quiet state. Some of the staff were already here and warming up in the ballroom. She changed into her dance shoes and sat back to observe but her mind wasn't really in the room at all. She was still in her dream about Edward's last few weeks. It was too peaceful to be dragged from that state of mind just yet. She contently let Suzanna lead the practice and simply stood with her partner in the center of the group and took orders.

Suzanna had them run through the choreography without music a few times so they could find their spacing on the floor. She watched them run through with music then rearranged the couples placing those who were stronger with their movements in the front. The newer staff members found the routine to be confusing in places, so she went over the tricky spots and carefully explained the intent of the step and how to better execute the lead or follow.

"Give me help on this hip up part!" Becca screamed with frustration as she managed to lunge down to the ground but couldn't get herself up. Suzanna demonstrated and showed how to keep the body in an upright posture as the back leg pressed into the floor to balance the hip motion up toward the man. "Wow that's hard," one of the downtown studio women remarked as they all tried the step with the new correction on positioning.

It was beginning to look better when they took a break to look at the costume situation. The Cally dresses were pulled from the closet and tried on for fit and color.

"I know these things can feel uncomfortable...," Suzanna tried to prepare them for the fit.

"Uncomfortable?" Anna Smith moaned. "These are downright unbearable." She was tugging and twisting her top to fit her ample chest.

"We need to try the whole routine a few times with them on, so when you get one that fits OK let's run through the dance with music again." Suzanna tried to help them adjust the skirts and find a suitable length for each one.

The first time through was so comical that Suzanna couldn't help but laugh as she watched from Edward's favorite spot behind his bongo drums. "Wow, we need to try that one again," she finally said when she could control her composure. "They really do make the routine look good though. You'll see. It's more put together." The group turned to stare back at her in disbelief. "Really they do," she reinforced. Then under her breath she added, "But we could certainly use a few more rehearsals with the costumes before show time. Let's try it one more time." She said this last bit in a full and cheerful voice.

Downtown teacher Megan was dancing with Antoine Hawks to the left of center. Her short cut shiny mahogany hair and full red lips looked fabulous with the red Cally leotard and skirt. Megan was a woman right out of a Reuben's painting – full breasted with a tiny waist and ample hips. Her smile was magnetic to an audience and the costume color drew even more attention to her classic look. As she went into her ronde behind Antoine's back her heel caught in the Cally skirt fold and she crashed ungracefully to the floor. There was a moment of silence. She didn't move but lay flat on her back eyes closed. As the group suddenly registered what had happened they began to crowd around, Antoine kneeling next to her trying to push the others back to give her space and a bit of air.

Mary Lou was pushing to squeeze past Lee and Kenneth Andrews but both were so tall that she was overpowered by their size. Finally peeking between them she saw Megan open her eyes and let out a loud gasp.

"Thank the Lord!" Mary Lou called out closing her eyes and raising her hand to the ceiling. When she opened her eyes she noticed everyone was staring at her, and she let out a heavy breath.

IX.

Kenneth Andrews was a puffy looking blond who stood a bit over six feet tall. His hair had no shape whatsoever and frequently flopped over the top of his black rimmed glasses. Just like all of the other male teachers, he wore a suit and tie to work but when the day was over he was just as quickly into casual clothes. He fancied himself not just a ballroom dancer but also a jazz dancer who stayed after work hours to flit and sway around the room to alternative music trying new and different poses and movements. Staring into the mirrors, he would move his mouth into a pout after each step and take a second to view himself.

"What do you think about this one?" he would call out to whoever was passing through. Most often times that someone would be Mary Lou Smith who was frequently the only one not racing out the door as soon as the clock hit ten o'clock. She would mumble something and walk across the small ballroom in her comfortable shoes to her office trying her hardest to ignore his odd poses.

Tonight was different. Charlotte who usually made a positive and encouraging comment to Kenneth had already told him how much she enjoyed the sequence he was working on. Then she was gone probably picked up by James. Kenneth continued his leaping sequence and waited for Mary Lou to venture out her door for a reaction. This time when she came out he asked the usual, "What do you think about this?"

Mary Lou stopped and instead of mumbling said, "Could you show me that again?"

Kenneth pulled back in shock, but then did the pattern again. "I like it," Mary Lou commented. "It shows innovation and a nice flow from the high position of the leap to the lowering of that turn into the floor and back up to a stand. Very nice."

Kenneth smiled. "What's gotten into you lately? Suddenly you are so positive. Oh, I'm sorry not that you weren't positive before…".

Mary Lou smiled. "You can say that if you want to. I won't get angry. I guess I wasn't the nicest person to be around most of the time. I just feel sort of free. It's hard to explain. I don't know what it is exactly. But I had this experience…". Then she went on to tell him about her visit to the church.

Kenneth didn't laugh. He just nodded his understanding and watched as she walked on toward Edward's office.

Mary Lou hadn't been in Edward's office since they found the body after the Mambo party. It was time to get over this reluctance to clean out his office. She opened the door and flipped on the light. She scanned the desk in the center of the room and the gaudy swirling silver wall paper. The back wall was painted a solid color with the paper running along the side walls making the room look long and narrow even though it wasn't. It seemed somewhat stark compared to Edward's downtown office with its warmth and coziness. He hadn't really put anything personal on the walls or around the desk area in this office. It felt cold and lifeless. What an appropriate word she thought. Lifeless.

She walked in and took another look around from all areas of the room. She pulled out the draws in his desk. Most were empty but there were a few papers – contracts and signed papers in one drawer. Underneath the papers was a book. She pulled out the book and noticed it was a Bible. It wasn't the kind that was a handed down Bible from family member to the next generation. This one was brand new. Although it opened like a new book that was still stiff in the binding, there were a few places that were worn. Several places flopped opened quickly and had passages underlined. Mary Lou read from some of the chapters in Psalms that Edward had marked. They all were about thankful praises to God. So peaceful, she thought. She sat a long time reading until she noticed Kenneth standing at the door.

He was wearing a black flannel cap with the flaps pulled down over his ears and the strings to tie it dangling at his chin, a worn knit scarf of black and white stripes and a black pea coat. "Just wanted to let you know I'm leaving," he said. "And I wanted to say thanks for your critique. It was nice."

"It looked good Kenneth," Mary Lou smiled back. "You do a nice job of teaching your students. They really appreciate you."

Kenneth's face brightened. "You think so?" She nodded.

The Memorial Service was scheduled for the late morning with a luncheon to be served after by the women in the church. Mary Lou welcomed this time to come back to the church and sit in peaceful silence in the sanctuary. She came over with Suzanna a bit early with the other teachers coming as a group later. Mary Lou told Suzanna about her first visit to the church and the impression she had about Edward's new found faith. "I think it was a blessing that he found this peace before his death."

Suzanna went over some of the plans for the tribute party this evening. They would have a chance to practice the routine again this afternoon and get things set up for the guests who would arrive around seven. The service in the church had been planned by Edward's family, but the tribute in the studio was the brainstorm of the dance staff. Maybe there would be some time also to meet with Edward's children and ex-wife.

In the hallway, Suzanna and Mary Lou noticed a group of people moving closer toward them. Suzanna took steps toward the woman in the front and gave her a hug. It was Edward's ex-wife. Suzanna had spoken with her on the phone, and Mary Lou recognized her from photos. Those photos must have been very old because this woman was much older than Mary Lou remembered. She was tall and big boned with a chilling stare. Sizing her up next to Suzanna who was tiny and petite with a delicate appearance, Mary Lou felt this woman was certainly taller than Edward had been. Standing next to her was a carbon copy but a few inches shorter. No longer the little curly haired child in the photo on Edward's desk, this girl was just as round as her mother and very stocky. Her mousy dark hair was cut short and she wore a pair of heavy glasses on her scowling face.

"This must be Casey," Suzanna said extending her hand to the girl with a smile. The girl hesitated but shook Suzanna's hand then Mary Lou's as well. The hand was large and callused. Casey wore a black button down shirt and black trouser pants that looked as if she had just pulled them from a suitcase. Her black shoes resembled heavy hiking boots.

Behind her was a slender boy with a sparkling smile and a head of floppy hair. "Clive?" Suzanna asked extending her hand to him as well. He smiled and shook the hand with a delighted look on his handsome face.

Suzanna went on about how long it had been since she had seen them and what a sad occasion it was that brought them back together. She said all of the right things then stepped aside to let them take their seats in the front of the sanctuary. Funerals were always so dismal she whispered to Mary Lou as they watched the group walk down the carpeted aisle.

The service was very nice with the pastor saying wonderful things about Edward and his life. He mentioned how much Edward had done for the church volunteering his time to some special projects as of late. Mary Lou raised an eyebrow at this although no one else seemed to be surprised. "Where have I been?" was her thought as she shook her head. "What haven't I noticed?"

The organ was playing as they left the sanctuary for the large gathering room for the luncheon. The family stopped briefly to speak with several people along the way, so Mary Lou and Suzanna made their way to the hall. The room was a bustle of middle aged women putting bowls and crock pots of warm homemade hot dishes onto a long serving table. There were plates and napkins toward one end of the table with a few women in matching white starched aprons standing to the side to replace and replenish. This was Minnesota – the heartland of the Scandinavian Lutheran pot luck. Each dish oozed with noodles and sauces and meats – the typical hot dish. At the other end of the table were the rolls. Fat round and white with a browned top, these rolls were stacked in baskets and would soon be replaced by more baskets of the same. The desserts were pans of brownies, bars and cookies made by the women in the church.

Mary Lou looked reluctantly at the table but decided to dig in. Why miss out on an opportunity to sample such an array of different dishes. This was something she had dreamed about but not quite on this day when she needed to feel light and slim in her Cally royal blue dress with the slits and twists exposing more of her than she wanted shown. Oh, well.

She noticed Casey and Clive ushered to the front of the line. Casey filled her plate to the brim but Clive was more selective in his choices. Some of the teachers chose not to stay and had returned to the studio to rehearse a bit more on their own before the performance. So only a small group of staff members remained to sample the smorgasbord. The other people were students and members of the church.

Standing off to the side in a small receiving line were Edward's ex-wife and his parents along with his grandmother. His mother was short and round with a halo of tight curls that she must have passed on to her son. What little hair Edward had left that was his own was around the ears and back of his head. It was all frizzy curls that he had tried to blend with his array of toupees. He had several that were meant to show various lengths as if growing out before a hair cut. It worked most of the time except when he would stand in front of the mirrors in the studio to adjust them. A tug here and there at times when he thought no one was watching showed the annoyance he had felt if everything on his head wasn't just right.

His father was tall and stocky with a severe look on his face. His balding head had a few white hairs combed over the top as if to pretend it wasn't hairless. He was taller than Edward had been, and Mary Lou recalled that Edward had rarely spoken of his father. They had a falling out when Edward turned his energies to dancing. It must have seemed an odd occupation to his father that somehow caused a riff to separate them. Or maybe they had always been distant.

The grandmother was short like Edward's mother but very tiny and frail looking. She stooped slightly and used a cane to move. It must have been the mother's mother, Mary Lou surmised. She certainly didn't resemble the hulking father in any way.

After finishing their food, Suzanna gathered the remaining staff and directed them toward the receiving line to shake hands with the relatives. Clive had joined his mother but Casey was now sitting in the back of the room looking bored. She stretched her legs out and slumped in a folding chair with her arms crossed and her eyes staring at the floor. She didn't pay attention to anything in the room and the rest of the room seemed to avoid her as well.

Suzanna cheerfully extended an invitation to the parents to attend the tribute party later at the studio. "We will be performing a special routine choreographed by Edward. It is our way of paying tribute to Edward's amazing talents as a dancer," Suzanna explained with a lightness to her voice. Edward's father just stared at her as if he didn't hear a word, but his mother smiled and said they would be happy to attend. With that, the dancers left to return to the studio to prepare for the event.

The studio was an electric with busy energy. Everyone scurrying about to set and reset the tables, chairs and photos. A snack table was slid into a back corner as the routine music played over and over. Couples would move out to a spot onto the floor to run through certain parts of the routine, then retreat to a corner to discuss with others about the execution. No lessons had been scheduled that day so the atmosphere was busy but relaxed at the same time.

Edward's ex-wife would escort her children and in-laws into the studio for a tour before the event was actually scheduled to begin. It would give them a chance to look at the photos and discuss the future plans for the studio before guests would arrive. Suzanna and Mary Lou were both tense with anticipation of that visit. Suzanna had prepared the receptionist to watch for their arrival and prompted her to be extremely cheerful and outgoing. Not that she would have to say something like that, but it was good to remind everyone that Edward's death had put the whole studio on a potentially new future.

Their arrival began a titter of excitement among staff members. Suzanna promptly greeted them and began to show them around the studio and talk about the impact Edward had made on so many people. Mary Lou stood back and in her heart felt herself pray. The ex-wife followed Suzanna closely throughout the tour with Casey and Clive behind trailed by Edward's parents who glumly glanced around. They ended in Edward's office with the door opened. It didn't hold so many people comfortably so Casey stood outside the door with her grandfather.

Suzanna had wisely chosen not to serve punch with the memory of Edward's poisoning in the back of everyone's mind. So tiny bottles of iced water and lemonade were in a cooler next to the snack table. She settled the group in comfortable chairs in the reception area and brought beverages and a plate of vegetables and fruit to the small coffee table then left to put on some music.

The ex-wife wandered into the ballroom to watch the rehearsal and selected a chair at one of the small glass tables that circled one end of the dance floor. Mary Lou took this opportunity to start up a conversation with her. "I'm so sorry for your loss...", she began as she took a seat next to her. "I'm Mary Lou Smith, the manager of the suburban studio."

"Diane Garrett. I never remarried after our divorce. This studio is just as I remember it with a few updates," she smiled as she swept a hand toward the musical equipment in the corner. "I only saw it briefly of course. We split almost immediately after Edward decided to move to Minneapolis and start up the studio."

Mary Lou glanced at Clive and Casey seated in the reception area. Casey was stretched out as before with her arms folded across her chest and a sullen look. Clive was carrying on a lively conversation with his grandmother.

"Clive certainly has his father's smile and energy," Mary Lou commented.

Diane smiled. "Yes, Clive is all Edward. Casey isn't really Edward's biological daughter and it is quite evident I suppose." Diane went on to explain although it wasn't something that was necessary. "Edward and I knew each other from childhood and dated all through high school. We had what you might call an 'open relationship', and I got pregnant by someone else. Edward married me before Casey was born knowing she wasn't his child. But it didn't seem to matter. He doted on her from the time she was born. I didn't tell her about it until his death. I didn't think it really mattered. But with the distance between Minnesota and California their relationship was strained the past few years. Certainly not because Edward didn't try. He did. Casey was just a teenager who was going through fazes any typical teen goes through only without her father there to help her through. She's not really herself today. Probably the blow of his death and then finding out he wasn't really her father was too much. I should have waited I guess."

Diane Garrett's confession seemed to be what she needed at that moment. She didn't have too many others she could confide in at this time and Mary Lou made the perfect sounding board. "Casey is a high school senior and after graduation will be joining the army," Diane added. "Her choice."

Mary Lou gave a quick glance at the girl slumped in her chair with the dark framed glasses sliding down her nose and contemplated this person in the army. Yes, a good move she agreed. Her clumsy black boots almost put her in uniform already. She was certainly not a California beach girl.

Diane continued, "I can't see Casey showing much interest in a dance studio but Clive is his father's son. He might some day have an interest. I'm sure you will be glad to know that we've decided to keep the studios and let you run them as you have been doing. I know from my years with Edward that you and Suzanna were probably doing all the work anyway." At that she laughed. "We'll arrange some way to direct any profits toward Casey and Clive in the form of education funds. I'm hoping after a few years in the army, Casey will shed this dark and dreary mood and be ready for furthering her education. If not, she can take the money and run." Again she laughed.

Mary Lou felt her heart lighten. She hadn't realized that this cloud was hanging over her head until it was lifted. It felt good suddenly. She was actually smiling right along with Diane Garrett. "I know you'll enjoy the routine we are performing for this tribute to Edward. It was a truly magnificent piece that he choreographed a few years ago and is a showcase for his talent. I must get into my costume now, but thank you so much for the conversation." And off she scurried to the back teachers' office. The royal blue Cally outfit hung taunting her from the hanger.

The people were arriving. The music was playing and those who chose were dancing. About midway through the evening, Suzanna stood at the bongo drums and grabbed the microphone.

"Tonight we pay tribute to a man who inspired us all. A man who taught us to love the art of dancing. Edward Garrett was not a perfect man, but he had an energy that was boundless and what he put his heart into he did with 200% of his effort. He showed us how to love to move, to appreciate music, and to enjoy the two combined with all of our hearts. We the staff here at the studio invite you to view the photo collection we have on display showing Edward Garrett's life and love. And we also would like to pay tribute to this man by performing one of

Edward's own routines. He would have loved to see how much we all enjoyed learning and rehearsing his movements. And now without further ado, the studio staff doing the rope hustle."

The audience applauded as the staff in their colorful dresses and black tuxes swarmed the floor to stop at exactly the right spots. Suzanna turned on the music and the couples precisely moved together with large swirling arm movements and quick footwork through the stunning routine. Suzanna will swear it was flawless and the oohs and aahs seemed to indicate she was correct. Everything moved in perfect precision. When they hit their final pose, even Casey and her grandfather were clapping. It was impressive.

When the night wound down and the people began to trickle out the door, Suzanna and Mary Lou sat down with Diane Garrett, Casey and Clive to repeat what Diane had already informed Mary Lou as far as the future plans for the studio. This time, however, the intent to keep the studio functioning as it was seemed more sincere and exciting. They seemed to feel the vibrations and the impact the studio had on others. It was a from the heart attempt to preserve what Edward had dreamed about.

"We're going to return to California tomorrow, but we have to meet with the police in the morning about any news in solving Edward's murder," Diane said with a sadness in her voice. The reality was there was someone out there who wanted Edward Garrett dead. They wanted some answers. The years of separation and estrangement didn't change the need for a solution to his death.

X.

Mary Lou went to the studio in the suburbs the next day with a new spring in her step. Some of the worry that had plagued her was behind and she felt a renewed confidence in her future as a dancer and as a manager. Her mind was reeling with new ideas and plans for success. Nothing could bring her down today. She whistled as she passed the desk.

"Good morning Eloise," she chirped. Eloise was huddled behind the desk and peered over her reading glasses with a confused look as Mary Lou passed by. Eloise had stayed out in the suburban studio the evening before to answer phone calls and make appointments rather

86

than attending the tribute. The buoyant mood that others felt from the party hadn't trickled down to Eloise as yet.

Mary Lou made a dash for the bathroom in the back of the ballroom. There were two small bathrooms marked "Gents" and "Ladies" tucked away in the back hallway that led to the exit door at the back of the large ballroom. She yanked opened the door to the one marked "Ladies" and found a figure hunched over the toilet.

It was Becca, her dark hair wrapped around the toilet seat with her head tilted down. She was making retching sounds and shaking as she grabbed the stool with her arms.

"Becca? Are you sick? What's the matter honey?" Mary Lou stood still not knowing whether to kneel down to help her or back out of the doorway and leave her to deal with her heaving alone.

Becca tilted her head back and looked at Mary Lou with watery eyes and a white as a ghost face. "I'm all right. I need to talk to you about something."

"If you're sick you should go home, and we'll reschedule your appointments. You don't look well at all." Mary Lou placed a hand on her shoulder to reassure her that a solution was in sight.

Becca stood and faced Mary Lou holding her stomach with one hand and wiping her mouth with a paper towel with the other. Becca stood a few inches above Mary Lou and sniffed. "I guess it would come out pretty soon any way. I'm pregnant."

"What? Who's the father? How did this happen?" The words came rapidly as Mary Lou unleashed a furry of short questions without waiting for an answer.

"I can't tell you. Or won't tell you." Becca said defiantly.

"Oh my god, it's Edward isn't it?" Mary Lou pulled back and shuddered.

Becca's face twisted into a repulsed gasp. "No! It's not Edward!" She thought for a moment and then confessed. "I guess it doesn't matter if you know or not. It's certainly better than thinking I could ever get involved with Edward Garrett. I met a man... a very famous man. He's an entertainer, a singer. I guess I was flattered by his attention to me and we spent time together for a few days while he was in town. Now he's gone and doesn't even remember who I am. I'm just one of many I'm sure. I was so stupid." Once again she started to gag and turned toward the toilet. Mary Lou looked away to give her some privacy and to avoid feeling sick herself.

"Well does he know about this?"

"Certainly not! And he's never going to find out." Becca reacted with a determined voice. "I will never tell him. Ever. And no one will ever know who he is either."

Mary Lou thought about Casey and finding out as a young adult that her father was not who she thought he was. She remembered the devastated look on her face the entire time she was at the studio. Was this the way Becca's unborn child would also face the world – not knowing and never finding out until something like a funeral brought out the truth? It was such a strange parallel.

"Well let's talk about this when you feel better. Do you want Eloise to cancel your appointments today?" Mary Lou felt a strange sorrow in the pit of her stomach for Becca.

"No. I'll feel better by afternoon. Really I will. But let's talk about this maybe tomorrow when I've thought through some things. I'm just glad to get over telling you, that's all. It's a big relief." Becca turned back toward the toilet, and Mary Lou closed the door gently giving her a bit of privacy.

Mary Lou sat in her office with the door closed. One teacher down. She had just begun to enjoy the thought of success and now she was dealing with a setback. Jilli and Charlotte were both teaching way too much to put Becca's students into their schedules. What to do? What to do?

She picked up the phone. "Suzanna? I may have a teaching spot to fill here. Do you have any trainees who are ready to teach?"

XI.

Further conversations with Becca shed no further light on who the father of her child might be. All she would say was he was "very, very famous". Finally, Mary Lou didn't attempt any more prying questions and just let it be. It wasn't any of her business anyway. In the back of her mind she pondered the effects this situation would have on her staffing at the studio. It took such a long time to train and integrate a new teacher into the ballroom teaching system. That point nagged her and as she responded by ignoring as best she could the implications of those thoughts, she felt the whole situation begin to consume her spirit and drive.

Mary Lou tried to release some of the pressure of studio life by taking a short stroll through the small mall each day during her lunch break. Peering in through the doors of the other stores and gazing at the displays of well put together outfits and gleaming jewels put her into a different world. She had her eye on a smart looking suit in the petite shop at the far end. She imagined how the teal blue color would highlight her eyes and draw out the color in her cheeks. The walk down there each day relieved the tension of the past week allowing her into a dreamy peaceful world that lasted maybe fifteen minutes. She gazed for a bit longer than usual and then reluctantly headed back to the studio. The studio music was playing in the background but no one was at the desk or on the floor. Mary Lou hesitated and slowed as she came to the Edward's office door. Glancing quickly and spotting no one she opened the door and shut it behind her. The office was still and dark. With no windows in the studio, the blackness was suffocating. She flipped on the light and listened for a stir out in the lobby, but there was nothing. Pulling open Edward's drawers she touched the Bible he had in the top drawer. It was still there. No one from the family had claimed it just as she expected. It was after all a new paperback version that had no sentimental value. Stopping only briefly to touch the glistening cover, she snatched it up and put it under her sweater. Then shutting off the light, she waited a moment to listen at the door and when she again heard nothing, she opened the door and stepped out into the brightly lit lobby. Eloise was just ambling back from the bathroom but her googly eyes were focused on the floor. She didn't notice Mary Lou until she was almost to the desk.

"Uh, do you need your schedule?" Eloise' voice squeaked. She was sausaged into a short black dress that revealed a few rolls around her waist and too tight pumps that seemed to expand her ankles uncomfortably. Whenever Mary Lou came around, Eloise seemed to be in a state of nervousness like a mouse cornered by a glaring cat. Not that Mary Lou tried to look anything but impatient when confronting Eloise. The woman was clearly annoying. Why Edward had ever decided she would man the front desk was a mystery to Mary Lou.

"Maybe just a quick glance…", Mary Lou peeked over the top of the desk to the large sheet flattened behind. All the while she gripped the Bible under her sweater hoping Eloise wouldn't notice the odd way she was clutching her sweater to her body. Then she hurriedly turned and a scampered back to her office. Her day looked relatively open. Normally something like that would alarm her, but today she pulled out the Bible, laid it on her desk with a marking pen, and began to read underlining passages that seemed to create a restlessness inside her stomach. Is this how Edward felt when he had read this? She noticed certain pages were worn – others untouched and stiff. The pages revealed something about Edward and his final days to her. And this made her a little uncomfortable. It was as if she were prying into his soul.

The day passed quickly and Mary Lou all but forgot about Becca and her dilemma. Instead she was so into her reading that she almost forgot to interview Kenneth's evening appointment. He had to rap on her door to remind her of the time. This was unusual but he seemed to pass over the situation easily enough. Mary Lou scratched out a few passages that she wanted to ponder on a piece of paper to take home with her that evening. She wanted very much to make sure she kept Edward's Bible at the studio. That somehow made the pick up from his drawer OK. After all, it was really still here and not taken or anything she rationalized. She wondered how Edward with some of his questionable habits had justified his actions after reading some of these passages. Then again wasn't she doing the same thing by justifying taking Edward's Bible as just "borrowing"? She vowed to put the Bible back after she had read everything.

Throughout the week, Mary Lou felt a comfort and calmness as she continued to read and delve into the new religion she had recently found. But she also found she snapped more quickly to judgment when dealing with others. One meeting she had found herself pointing accusingly at Kenneth and telling him he lived a "vile disgusting life". It had come out of nowhere really. He had mentioned something he had done the evening before at a bar Mary Lou knew was a gay hangout. She tried to hold herself back but all the words just gushed forth. Kenneth had looked at first shocked then he simply pulled himself into an invisible ball and had not participated any more in that meeting. His mopped blond head lowered as his glasses slid down to the end of his nose and all but disappeared into his folded arms resting on the table top. His hunched shoulders rolled forward and he looked like a turtle pulling into its shell. She knew she should apologize, but she didn't. She just let the incident fester.

The next day she had berated Becca in front of the others. Becca's secret had not been formally announced and wouldn't, but Mary Lou suddenly jumped on her with such anger – "If you didn't lead such a sinful lifestyle you would have all that you set for your goals, you know." That had been the beginning of her tirade as they went over daily and weekly goal sheets. The rest of the comments shall remain unsaid.

Charlotte had quite calmly stepped between Mary Lou and Becca, taking Mary Lou's arm and pulling her back into her office. Then after firmly closing the door and pressing her tall thin frame against the door for a moment, Charlotte motioned for Mary Lou to take her seat behind her desk. Mary Lou meekly sat but was taken back by the words she heard.

Charlotte's tanned slender arm swung gracefully from the silken patterned fabric that swirled around her body in loose folds. She wore one of her own creations that would look hideous on someone like Eloise or even Mary Lou, yet on Charlotte seemed to float and draw attention to her fluid body lines. "You are a baby," she began. "A baby Christian who like so many before you are taking your new found lifestyle and viewpoints to find faults in everyone else. Religion is not about digging up sin in others. You will never be effective as a manager, a leader, or as a Christian until you recognize that faith is not about evil, but about new life and love for others." Charlotte spoke deliberately yet kindly. Her voice was soft and soothing with a light high pitch.

Mary Lou was taken back by the direct understanding in Charlotte's words. It was as if she really knew what she was talking about, although Mary Lou had felt all week that she, Mary Lou was the only one who knew the secrets of this book – Edward's Bible. What did Charlotte know anyway?

Charlotte continued, "You will find at first that it is easy to point accusing fingers at people who have made choices you have not, but after you feel comfortable with your faith you will find that it is not your duty to find the 'speck in your brother's eye and ignore the log in your own'." Mary Lou marveled at Charlotte's ability to quote scripture so appropriately. "I had this conversation many times with Edward before he died…".

Mary Lou's head lifted abruptly with a start. "Yes," Charlotte leaned forward with slight smile on her face, "I knew Edward was finding his soul. And he was having difficulty with much that was going on inside of him before his death. We spoke often about the transformations he was feeling and the lifestyle choices he needed to change. He reacted much the same you are – always wanting someone else to 'see the light'. But he recognized there was more about himself needing to adjust, and he quickly stopped picking apart others. I am sure I was one he originally wanted to change. That's how we started our conversations about his new religion. My faith has been strong for a long time now. And by the way so has Becca's. She is going to have to deal with a lot of things – yes, I know about her pregnancy. Her parents and church friends are not going to be as kind about the situation as we should be. We should be her support and not her accusers. That's what she needs right now. Friends."

Charlotte's voice trailed off, and Mary Lou sat with a sudden heaviness inside. Who was she to accuse anyone? After all, she was one person who should know how it feels to be accused of something. She was still the prime suspect in Edward's murder. She wanted tears to roll down her face. She wanted her remorse to show, but nothing happened. It was as if she had an empty hollow body with only stale air filling the void.

"If you need someone to talk to about things…", Charlotte's soothing tones split the silence. Mary Lou watched her turn to leave, then suddenly called out. "Wait! Please wait." Her voice pleaded – begged.

Hoarsely she continued, "Could you help me find Edward's real murderer? I can't bear this burden of guilt anymore." Then hesitating she added, "And could you ask Becca to come into my office?"

Charlotte looked over her shoulder and her lips turned slightly into a thin lipped smile. "Yes, of course. To both requests." Then she left to find Becca.

The next half hour was not easy for Mary Lou. She and Becca talked about everything – apologies, support for each other, what the studio needed to prepare for, what Becca and Mary Lou needed to prepare for. The talk seemed endless but by the time Becca's first student of the day paced nervously for his lesson in the waiting room, much had been resolved. Becca was her usual sparkling self, and Mary Lou was better – yes, better was the right word.

The calm was short lived, however. It was about 4:30 in the afternoon just before the evening mad rush of students would send all of the teachers out to the dance floor for a flurry of lessons when Lee Watkins rushed into the reception area. He looked pale and was stuttering uncontrollably. "Call the police," he demanded staring at Eloise behind the desk. Eloise, eyes bugging out sat frozen as he started to scream. Mary Lou and Charlotte came running from their offices, and Kenneth raced out from the back ballroom where he was practicing a few dance moves for the evening group class.

"What's going on?" someone said. No one knew exactly what happened from that point on, but Lee explained with sheer panic on his face that he and Jilli Wilson had been carjacked. They were sitting in a fast food parking lot waiting to pick up their meals when a man had put his fist through Lee's rolled down window. In his fist was a gun. He had ordered Lee out of the car and had sped off with Jilli still in the passenger's seat. Lee had run all the way back to the studio. By this time, Eloise had composed herself enough to call the police and a squad car pulled up within a few moments.

Lee went over his story again for the two officers as one of the uniformed men put out a quick call to look for Lee's car. The rest of the studio staff sat back trying to fade into the background. The tension was like a heavy fog covering the reception area in a blanket. Lee's face was contorting in pain as he tried to describe the man who had abducted Jilli. His curly mass of hair was damp and his hands shaking. There was a tear in his shirt collar and his colorfully patterned tie hung to the side of his neck in long, crumpled disarray.

Mary Lou and Charlotte sat in the background on one of Edward's low slung psychedelic couches clinging to each other, each wanting to go over to hold Lee and

99

comfort him. They knew that wouldn't help at this point and waited for him to give all the information to the police so Jilli could be found. "Please keep her safe," they prayed in whispers to each other clinging to each others hands.

The vision of a terrified Jilli crouching against the car door was almost too much for Lee to take, and he broke into tears as he described the scene in as much detail as he could muster while the police radios chattered back and forth hiding the sobs he made. He pictured her honey colored hair swinging back from her face and her tanned legs curling up in front of her as the gunman stuck the weapon in her face. He told the policeman the holdup man was white with a navy hooded sweatshirt, baggy jeans, and basketball shoes. He looked to be in his late teens or early twenties. The man had a stubble of growth on his face that couldn't be a beard really. Just hadn't shaved in a day or two. The description was classic yet clear. It could be anyone or no one. Could they find the car? Had too much time elapsed from the time of the carjacking to the arrival of the police? How far could the driver travel in that time?

Kenneth and Becca leaned on the top of the desk gazing in disbelief at the scene. Kenneth's white blond hair flopped uncontrollably into his eyes as he cradled his face in the palms of his hands. Becca's usual toothy grin had turned to an unbecoming frown and a furrowed brow creased into a face of worry. This day had been trying in every way for her personally, and she backed up uneasily to slide into a sea foam green stackable chair sitting in the corner of the small ballroom.

A crackling sound from the police radio prompted the office to cover one ear and move out to the hallway and then out to the parking lot. The mall didn't attract a crowd of people normally, but the appearance of the squad car with its light flashing out on the curb had brought some on lookers who were gawking in hopes of finding out what was happening. The officer pulled himself away from those craning their necks to see something. After a moment that felt like an eternity to those in the studio reception area, he returned. "They've found the car," he reported. "That's all I can tell you at this point."

There was a heaving sigh from Lee. Charlotte and Mary Lou embraced briefly. "Would you like to come with us, sir," the officer continued speaking to Lee who continued to gaze up waiting for more news. "I can't really tell you much more at this point, but I think you might want to be present when we receive a report."

"Yes," Lee gasped. "Yes, I would like to go with you, please." He rose and followed them out turning briefly to give the rest a look that seemed to say "I'll call you as soon as I know anything."

The news came later. Eloise had already cancelled Jilli and Lee's appointments for the evening. All the others could really do was try to carry on as if nothing had happened, teaching their lessons and acting as if everything was wonderful. But something was very wrong and the evening felt like a nightmare.

When Lee called, Eloise transferred the call quickly to Mary Lou's office. Charlotte excused herself from her lesson leaving her student standing in the middle of the floor and joined Mary Lou. With the speaker phone on, Lee told them that the car had been found, and Jilli and the attacker had still been in the car when the police surrounded the vehicle. She had been sexually attacked and beaten but the man had been arrested quickly and without incident once the car was located in a remote parking lot a few blocks from the fast food restaurant. Jilli was recovering in the hospital. Lee's voice was shaking. He would stay at the hospital over night to make sure Jilli was as comfortable as possible. She might be staying a few days, he reported.

"She looks pretty bad," Lee choked out. "Her face is starting to bruise. She must have put up a good fight that he would hit her like that." His voice crackled as he described the cuts and black eye Jilli had sustained. "She's still beautiful though. Beautiful."

The hospital where Jilli had been taken was only a short distance from the studio. Mary Lou and Charlotte had quickly gathered up their purses and leaving Eloise with a few instructions had climbed into Mary Lou's little compact car for the drive. They both knew without saying anything to each other that Lee needed someone there more than Jilli needed a few extra visitors.

Outside of the door to Jilli's room, Lee and Jilli's mother waited. Lee was on one side of the room and her mother was huddled in the corner on the other side. Lee nodded to Mary Lou and Charlotte as they scurried from the elevator to the small area cluttered with uncomfortable low backed chairs and stacks of old magazines.

"The police are in with her now. They wanted to interview her as quickly and soon as possible so she could rest and get some medication," Lee explained in a low voice. "This is Jilli's mom...". He introduced them to the blond woman clinging to her corner chair. She didn't really look like Jilli. The blond hair was too platinum in color and had the start of dark roots showing at the middle part. Short and stocky, the woman seemed to be in a state of shock. She looked past Mary Lou and Charlotte as if they weren't even there at all. Her unfashionable stretch pants and baggy sweater seemed to be from another decade.

Mary Lou and Charlotte hesitated for a moment looking at each other as if to telepathically ask the other what they should do. Then without a moment's hesitation, Charlotte walked over to Jilli's mother and sitting down next to her put her arms around the woman. Mary Lou retreated to Lee and put her hand on his shoulder as if to reassure him that they had come for him as well as Jilli.

The doctor came by and stopped to chat with the group. Introducing himself, he expressed his regret for this unfortunate situation and then recommended that only one person at a time visit Jilli limiting the visit to only five or ten minutes. She of course needed their support but also needed to get some rest. The medication they would be giving her would allow her to sleep. He also said he thought she might be able to go home the next day as her injuries at this point were not severe. His assessment made Mary Lou feel a little better. But she had not seen Jilli yet. And when she did, it felt shocking.

Allowing Jilli's mom to go in first was of course the proper thing in everyone's mind. Then Lee had his turn. When he came out he was worse then when he had gone in.

"If only I had fought back. If only I hadn't been such a coward..." he muttered to himself placing all of the blame for the incident on himself.

Mary Lou was not looking forward to her short visit. And it was worse than she had anticipated. Jilli's lip was puffy and beginning to bruise as was her eye. She had been hit in the face probably more than once. Jilli Wilson was a sun goddess in every sense of the description. She was tall, lean and tanned with the look of young deer – wide eyed and innocent yet worldly at the same time. She supplemented her dance income with modeling. Photos of her wrapped in swim suits and clingy skirt wraps graced many fashion catalogues. The glossy pictures seductive yet fashionable drew the customer to her lightly streaked golden deep honey hair flowing back from her face and blowing around her shoulders. Her soft brown eyes gazed back at the camera with only a touch of make up giving her a natural outdoor quality that was truly unique in the fashion world. Now she was huddled in the corner of her bed with a frightened yet angry cast in her eyes.

Mary Lou's attempts to be light and humorous failed miserably. She soon was left with nothing more to say than a brief apology and the assurance that they would all be there for her. She left with a sinking feeling in her stomach only to come face to face with…Jilli Wilson.

Charlotte was sitting in the middle of a group of women – Jilli's mother and three other women. One was Jilli Wilson. The group was in conversation going over details of the abduction and the medical reports. Lee was no where to be seen.

For the moment no one noticed Mary Lou backed into the corner of the room. The Jilli person was saying something strange. "First I have to witness Edward Garrett's murder scene and now this. What is it with this studio? It gives me the creeps."

Charlotte looked up with a startled look as she spotted Mary Lou. "Oh, Miss Smith. This is Jilli's family. Her sisters. Joni, Jessica and Jordan."

The Jilli look alike held out her hand and noticing the look of confusion on Mary Lou's face explained, "I'm Joni, Jilli's twin sister."

Mary Lou's look of surprise softened. "Twin sister? My but you two look alike."

Joni had the same honey hair and tanned lanky look. But she seemed to dress frillier somehow. She wore a silky layered skirt with a ruffle around the bottom and a lacy blouse with full puffy sleeves. This was definitely

106

something that Jilli would never wear. Jilli was one to wear something sleek and classic in basic color tones and not this flowery fabric. But if you only saw the face, you would swear that it was Jilli Wilson herself. The sisters whispered back and forth for a moment before deciding that Jessica would go in for a visit first. Jessica was the oldest sister, tall and thin like Jilli and Joni but with a hardened sun baked face that showed no softness in its features as the twin's faces did. She wore a business suit in a dark cold color with no jewelry or scarf for color accent. The second oldest, Jordan remained seated next to their mother holding her hand and gazing into her tear streaked face. Jordan was matronly like the mother - smaller and round with a fleshy face and clothes that looked outdated and well worn. Mary Lou had noticed the medication the doctor had given Jilli was starting to take effect as she left the room, so she didn't think there would be much chance that Jilli would be awake for these next few visits. But sisters would certainly want just to sit by her bed and assure themselves that she was going to be OK.

"Are you close?" Mary Lou asked Joni. "I don't know that I've seen you around the studio at all."

Joni looked a bit startled by this last question and hesitated before answering. "Well, actually I have been into the studio." She hesitated again and looked to Charlotte. Charlotte said nothing but nodded her head indicating that she should explain further. "OK," Joni said, "here's the deal. I was at the studio the night Edward was killed. I was at the party."

Mary Lou now standing sat back into her chair and waited for the rest of the story. Joni continued, "Jilli did the staff routine but had a modeling gig that night. So as soon as the routine was done, we switched places. She left and I entered wearing the clothes she had on originally so everyone would think she was still there. I saw you and Edward standing at the punch bowl talking. Then I slipped by you and sort of hung out in the large ballroom. No one else knew except Charlotte here who knew something was a bit off. I tried to avoid dancing. And of course Lee figured out something was up when I totally ignored him. But then with the murder and all, no one really paid much attention to me. I told the police I was Jilli Wilson and left. Went home. Lee doesn't know I was there so don't let on. OK." Then she added something with a coldness in her voice, "I knew Edward Garrett. He approached me several times thinking I was Jilli."

It was becoming easier for Mary Lou to see the difference in the two women. Jilli was completely different than Joni except for the resemblance in the face and body type. They had completely different personalities and manner of speech. It was actually quite mind boggling to even think that earlier she thought they were the same person now that she had heard Joni speak.

"I suppose I should tell the police...", Joni looked down at the floor and hesitated to look Mary Lou in the face. "Not that it would make any difference. Because I didn't kill him and I don't know who did." And that was that.

XII.

When Mary Lou returned to the studio, she shut herself in her office. Running over the events of the day was difficult. There were too many things to think about. Charlotte had said that Lee was a basket case. He felt responsible for the whole incident and knew that Jilli would blame him for what had happened to her. Jilli Wilson had been just about the best thing to happen to him. She was beautiful and talented and really was the first woman to pay much attention to him at all. Mary Lou knew this to be true. She remembered when Lee was a student. Suzanna

Caldwell had been his teacher. Taking the shy just out of high school boy with the angelic face and halo of curls, teaching him to not only dance but to excel in something had been life changing. Then when he became a part of the staff and met Jilli Wilson, his life was the dream he had always imagined it would be. He was admired by others and had women thinking he was "amazing". Now today had broken that world in two. How would he cope with this day?

Mary Lou picked up the phone and called Suzanna. She retold the events of the day, leaving out the part when Charlotte had lectured about Mary Lou's new religious fervor. She told her about Becca and her pregnancy, about the abduction and finding of Jilli Wilson, and about Jilli's twin sister. "She was in the studio when Edward was killed," Mary Lou blurted out at the end.

"My, my," was all Suzanna could say. Mary Lou could imagine that at this moment Suzanna was holding the phone with one hand and covering her mouth with the other hand. This was Suzanna's normal reaction to anything surprising or thought provoking. There was silence and Mary Lou let the tale sink in. "My, my."

"I need a teacher quickly for a few days to take Jilli's students and possibly to take over for Becca. When

Becca starts to show it will become a problem. Especially in this business. I know it sounds sexist, but dancing is too physical for someone to put in as many hours as we do and with all of the activity, if the teacher is uncomfortable, well, it just doesn't service the student properly." Mary Lou knew she was making excuses. She really didn't want to explain to a new student why their teacher looked like she had swallowed a watermelon and wasn't married. "Married" was a term the dance business didn't recognize. This was a business for youth and not the mature family person. At least at this time it was. Mary Lou hoped that would change in the future as she moved closer to the husband and family era in her own life.

"Let me see if I can send you Sydney Monroe," Suzanna was hesitating as she remained in deep thought.

"I was hoping maybe you could spare Anna...". Mary Lou's sister Anna was just the person she needed at this point. Anna was not only a magnificent dancer, but she was someone Mary Lou could confide in. And a confidant was someone she needed desperately. She knew her voice sounded a bit whinny so she bit her lip and decided not to say much more.

"Sorry, honey, but Anna is all booked up. I can't spare her right now. But Sydney. Well, I could move her students to other teachers. Divide them out for now and it would work out. Sydney is a great dancer, and I'm sure your studio would love her!" Suzanna was upbeat and enthusiastic.

Yeah, Mary Lou knew that Sydney would work out. OK, if she had to have someone other than Anna, Sydney Monroe would do. Sydney was Anna's closest rival in the advanced teaching department at the downtown studio so always gave Mary Lou a somewhat sour stomach when she thought of her moving in on Anna's territory. This was a business after all and your students represented your income. Anna had been in her own little world the past few years with no one biting at her heels until Sydney had shown up and began the nipping. Mary Lou knew she shouldn't have this animosity for Sydney, and now she would have to curb that feeling of rivalry to work with her. It would make or break the studio in this increasingly difficult situation if Mary Lou continued to hold a grudge. She hung up the phone and went up to the front desk to tell Eloise what to do with all of the appointments.

Eloise just stared at her when she explained that Sydney would be taking Jilli's students for the next week at least. Eloise was to call each one and without telling them what had happened, let them know they would have a substitute teacher. "Tell them she's sick or something. Not exactly a lie. Hopefully they don't put something in the paper with her name so we have to field question." Mary Lou was becoming frustrated with the whole situation as she imagined what might happen in the future. Would Jilli come back in a week? Would she come back at all or was she too traumatized by the assault? "You haven't told anyone yet, have you?" Mary Lou suddenly began to notice Eloise's eyes bulge out like they did when she was guilty of something. Eloise seemed particularly nervous about this whole Jilli Wilson event.

Eloise stammered slowly, "No...no." She told someone Mary Lou guessed. Maybe more than one person. This was going to get out and everyone would be talking. Wow, won't Jilli feel great when she comes back with everyone staring and whispering? Mary Lou glared at Eloise but said nothing more.

Sauntering back to the large ballroom, Mary Lou pulled out a covered dance program to prepare for her 9:00 lesson. Although Mary Lou usually never taught lessons herself since taking on the management position at the new studio, she had somehow accumulated one lone student, Max Krinkie. One evening Eloise had frantically rushed into Mary Lou's office with a problem. They had double booked Jilli Wilson with two new students. What should they do? Mary Lou had angrily declared she would take the one student and teach him the introductory lesson herself, and Eloise had slunk back to the front desk with a mixture of relief and humiliation. Max Krinkie had proven to be an ideal student and rather than pass him off to another teacher after the introductory lesson was over, Mary Lou kept teaching him booking him each week at the same 9:00 slot. She actually found herself looking forward each week to the lesson with Max.

Max sat in the reception area smiling at all of the students coming in and going out. He had become a favorite of everyone else as well. He was young and personable. Only a bit taller than Mary Lou with an athletic build and clean cut look, he had taken to dancing like a fish to water. His family owned a shoe store over at the large mall across the street and when people began coming in to request dance shoe orders and repairs to the soft soles of the glittery shoes they already had, Max became curious and had stopped in to try a little of the dancing his customers were raving about. It had become addicting and soon was a weekly part of his social life.

Mary Lou motioned for him to follow her into the large ballroom and wordlessly they began to warm up with a smooth Waltz. Max easily led Mary Lou through a series of box steps and turns and then began to move effortlessly around the floor with twinkles and spirals. Mary Lou may not have shown it at that moment, but she was proud of the progress her student had made with his dancing. His command of the patterns and various dance styles was impressive. People always seemed to stop their own dancing to watch the two of them. Tonight was no exception. The edge of the floor was lined with students gazing at the progress Max made around the line of dance, leading Mary Lou into several sweeping and elegant movements. When they finished their warm up Waltz, someone began to clap and Max turned a slight shade of red.

"You'll never know how much I am looking forward to this lesson," Mary Lou confessed as she pulled out the lesson plan and proceeded to tell Max what they would be working on that evening. A new pattern in the Rumba along with some hip exercises to get a more natural Cuban motion. Then they would try a bit of Tango reviewing the new link they had learned last week. Max nodded and smiled. Mary Lou knew the best way to teach a lesson: enthusiasm, compliment, new material, and review.

Charlotte stopped and watched the progress of Max and Mary Lou's Tango as she escorted her own student to the reception area at the finish of their lesson. Charlotte and Mary Lou leaned on the front desk counter watching Max leave the studio after his lesson surrounded by a group of women students. His faded blue jeans and long sleeved t-shirt was fashionably accented with his dance shoe bag slung over his shoulder. After Max had walked out the door, Charlotte whispered in Mary Lou's ear. "You might consider asking Max to join the staff." Mary Lou's head jerked to the side, and she gazed thoughtfully into Charlotte's animated face. As Charlotte raised her eyebrows she reminded Mary Lou that Lee might not be himself for a while and another male staff member might be nice for everyone. Then she walked off leaving Mary Lou to ponder another staff addition. It was all so exhausting. The studio was so new that they had not had any staff changes except for the empty office left by Edward's murder. Nothing had changed in the studio other than Edward and now it was rolling in all directions. Mary Lou was not emotionally prepared for change, but she would have to get her mind into accepting what would be inevitable. There would be change.

The next day was as much as a disaster as the day before but in a different way. Instead of all of the quick emergencies experienced the prior day, Eloise had managed to mangle all of the moved appointments. Lee had called in to say he wasn't planning to come in. No surprise there, but trying to schedule his heavily booked day with only Kenneth was a bit tricky. Sometimes they would suggest an exchange lesson with another woman to work on arm styling and Latin motion. Mary Lou would have to be willing to accept some exchange lessons for a while. In her mind she quickly made a decision to call Max later and ask him to help them out as a "teacher in training". She knew he would be working during the day in his family's business, but if he could spare a few hours in the evening they might just get through this situation in a smoother manner than they were currently. Eloise was no help at all. She didn't seem to know what to tell any of the students when she called them to change appointment times, and she seemed more distracted than usual if that were even possible.

"Just call me off a lesson if you have to and let me talk to the person," Mary Lou had finally told her angrily. Sydney came in for the early afternoon meeting and seemed eager to take over as many lessons as possible.

Mary Lou had to admit she was a go getter. Maybe a go getter was what this studio needed at this moment. Sydney's smile was contagious and her way with words soothed even the most upset and complaining student. Mary Lou felt a sense of relief as she hurried back to her waiting student after one of Eloise's distraught pleas to take a phone call. She breezed by Sydney and said a little prayer of thanks. Maybe God did answer her prayer after all.

Soon the ballroom was buzzing with happy students, laughter, lively music, and a back to business atmosphere. Max had agreed to come in to take a few of Lee's students – at least the beginning students. Mary Lou was still a bit hesitant to let him teach the more advanced dancers. She didn't want him to become too overwhelmed and never come back. Maybe she could work out a system where he would join her in a lesson and do the dancing with the more advanced student and Mary Lou would do the teaching. That might work quite well. She found herself with a smile on her face – and it had been a long time since that had happened.

Mary Lou retreated at the end of the day to Edward's office and closed the door. Hiding in the quiet darkness with no one able to find her for a few moments was pure pleasure. She stood with her back against the door and closed her eyes. The door was directly across from the front desk and no one had been there when she slid through the door for her brief retreat. Now she could hear voices behind the door. It wasn't a voice she recognized and the sounds were a bit muffled. She put her ear to the door and tried to understand more of the conversation.

Eloise Parker was saying,..."But sweetie, I need this job. It's important I stay here so I can..." then the next part was muffled. The voice responding back was a man's. Ben? Her young boyfriend? It must be. He must have come to pick her up after work. Was he concerned that Eloise might be in danger because of the incidents with Edward's murder and Jilli's attack? They certainly weren't related, were they? It was just bad luck. That was all. Strange bad luck.

"I have to keep my ears opened so..." again Eloise was talking and fading off. Then Ben said something about Jilli Wilson. So it did have to do with the Jilli incident that was causing his concern. Maybe she should just go out and tell him there was nothing to worry about. It had nothing to do with anyone else in the studio – it was random – a stranger who had abducted Jilli. Besides, they had the man who was involved. He was in jail right now. Nothing to be concerned with.

Mary Lou peaked out and saw the two with their backs to her starting to leave. She waited and a second later slid out without anyone noticing. Then she scurried to the front door to watch the couple slide into an old rusted car parked out front in the "No Parking" zone of the curb. Ben was still the same young kid she had remembered from their other brief visits. His thinning hair made him appear older at first, but she could see now that she watched him more closely that he had a youthful face and body. He had a scowl on his face and looked angrier than she remembered. Maybe he was really worried about the studio and unhappy that he had not been able to talk Eloise into quitting. That's all the studio needed at this moment – another person leaving or with a problem and unable to work. Mary Lou would have to make a point to be extra nice to Eloise, as hard as that might be. Replacing Eloise would not be something she wanted to do at this time.

"Just a quick call," Suzanna had said when Mary Lou picked up the studio phone as it rang on her way out the door. "Could we meet for breakfast tomorrow? There is something I need to talk with you about. Privately."

Mary Lou was curious as to what Suzanna needed to tell her. All night she was restless and not sleeping well. When morning finally arrived, she jumped in the shower and donned a skirt and blazer. Quickly drying her hair and putting on her make up, she arrived at the restaurant by Suzanna's apartment a bit early and ordered coffee.

Suzanna arrived early as well and slid into the booth in the back of the little café with a concerned look on her face. Ordering hot tea, a fruit cup and a cinnamon roll, Suzanna's face remained deep in thought. Apologizing, she explained after the food was ordered. "Sorry to keep you in suspense, but I want to sort out what I have to tell you first." Hesitating she continued as best she could, "As you know, the police seem to be more in contact with me about Edward's death than anyone else. I suppose they feel it inappropriate to call you if you happen to still be on their 'prime suspect' list." She laughed at her own joke then continued. "The man arrested for Jilli Wilson's abduction and assault claims he was hired to abduct her. He claims that someone called him and offered him money to abduct Jilli and get rid of her. He says he doesn't know who the person was who made contact with him. He's not a very reliable person needless to say – he has a long list of offenses on his record, so what he claims may or may not

121

be true. Again it could be a partial truth. He followed Jilli and Lee that afternoon with the intent of getting rid of her – whatever that may mean. But when he saw Jilli, he changed his mind and decided to sort of keep her around. She is a beautiful girl after all and I guess that saved her. At least it gave the police enough time to located them and arrest the man. The physical assault may have actually saved her life."

Mary Lou sat back in the booth and pondered the news. So Jilli Wilson's abduction was not random and could indeed be related to Edward Garrett's murder. That was a surprise. What does it all mean?

The food arrived and as hungry as Mary Lou had been before getting to the café, she now picked at her plate of eggs and sausage. Suzanna took a few sips of hot tea and then decided to throw out some additional thoughts.

"Well we now know that whoever killed Edward thought Jilli Wilson was a threat. I wonder how that could be. Especially if Jilli wasn't actually in the studio when Edward was killed. Maybe she heard something she shouldn't have or saw something. What are your thoughts here?" Suzanna went down her list of suspicions.

"I wonder if they took the wrong person," Mary Lou ventured slowly. "Maybe whoever killed Edward was fooled like the rest of us were and thought Joni Wilson was Jilli. Maybe Joni didn't even know who or what she saw that night. Maybe she was just there and that put Jilli in danger. That all means it was someone at the party that night – someone in the studio. Of course, we suspected that all along. But this surely makes the person much more dangerous than we originally thought. They were not satisfied with just murdering Edward. They decided to get rid of Jilli as well."

"Might I make a suggestion," Suzanna placed her hand over her mouth as she always did when she was a little surprised or toying with a thought. "We need to talk with Jilli and Joni to find out what they might have heard or seen. But you might not be the person to do the asking. You are after all, the management. We are the management. You and I being the bosses might not get the whole truth if we ask. How about sending Charlotte or Sydney in as sort of spies?"

Mary Lou was not surprised with the suggestion of Charlotte, but Sydney? Why did she mention Sydney?

"Charlotte is a good suggestion, but she is also someone involved in your studio. And it would appear that the person or persons involved is from your studio. Sydney is an unbiased outsider. Someone who the Wilsons might be more unguarded with in conversation. They might just say more, explain more, you know… go into more detail about something that is on their mind. Something that didn't seem important before. With Charlotte they might be more guarded because she is a teacher Jilli works with all the time." The suggestion seemed to make sense. Sydney was someone with an upbeat personality who seemed to easily get people to confide in her. There weren't many people in the studio left who qualified as suspects. The list was growing shorter. Of course, it could be a student. Someone who came into the studio each week and didn't seem connected but was. It was worth giving Sydney a shot. Mary Lou would have to confide in her and let her somehow draw out information not only from Jilli and Joni, but Charlotte, Becca, Kenneth and Lee.

"You know if the police let Jilli know what her captor said, she could take the news several ways," Suzanna pondered. "She might feel grateful and lucky that she is still alive. On the other hand, she may feel more frightened about coming back to the studio knowing she was an intended target. And hopefully the news will somehow absolve Lee of any involvement, unless he actually is involved. Maybe the killer targeted Jilli to force

Lee's hand because they knew Jilli to be an important person in his life."

"Too complicated!" Mary Lou didn't want to think about all of the implications of that whole situation. There were too many angles to this consider. Too many possibilities. She shook her head and vowed to have a talk with Sydney Monroe before the daily meeting today. Sydney now seemed to be their only hope for figuring out what had actually happened.

Mary Lou made it back to the studio in record time. Such were the perks for working a non conventional schedule. Traffic was always at a minimum. Eloise was plopped behind the front desk with her usual glum and confused look. Mary Lou made a point of complimenting her on her shocking hot pink mohair sweater and hideous flowered mini skirt. That seemed to soften her attitude a bit. She actually smiled.

"How do the appointments look for today? Did we get things arranged for most of the day?" Mary Lou tried to sound soothing in her approach. Eloise looked over the daily schedule and didn't answer back immediately.

"Here, let me take a look and see what we have," Mary Lou said calmly. She reached for the sheet and scanned the pencil scrawls. Even if she spotted a problem,

Mary Lou vowed not to make a mention to Eloise. Instead she smiled brightly at her and complimented her on her hard work with a difficult situation. "We can schedule Max Krinkie this evening starting about 6:00 with some of Lee's students. Just make sure if the student is more advanced that you also schedule me out on the lesson. He should do fine with that."

"When will Miss Wilson be back? Do we know yet?" Eloise tapped on the column reserved for Jilli. "Her students are asking questions."

"Well, at this moment I don't know. With Miss Monroe coming from the downtown studio to help out, we should be able to make do until we find out more about the situation. As a matter of fact, while I think about it, could you please ask Miss Monroe to meet with me in my office when she comes in? I would like to go over students and schedules. And ask Charlotte if she could start the meeting for me so I have enough time with Miss Monroe." It all seemed so simple and yet so sensible. Yes, it was quite natural to arrange things this way. No one need know the truth of the meeting. Eloise grinned happily at Mary Lou and seemed satisfied with the request. "Who knows if Miss Wilson will ever come back with the ordeal she has had to go through…", Mary Lou thought that last statement might be a good clincher. Leaving doubt that Jilli would return might mean a cushion of safety for her if by chance Eloise would happen to mention something about her condition to any of her students. Eloise would of course pass this tidbit of information on and hopefully to the right person. It might make them feel more secure – safer – and then maybe they would make a mistake. Mary Lou would be ready for a mistake. Ready for something out of the ordinary to pop out and give her the clue she needed.

A moment of prayer was just what Mary Lou needed at this moment. She recognized that her hostility for Sydney Monroe might complicate this meeting and she asked for the strength to put her differences behind her and move on with a positive attitude. Maybe the words of this simple prayer would bring a feeling of peace and allow a very productive conversation. As Mary Lou tightly pressed her eyelids closed, the door opened and Sydney Monroe entered, hesitated and waited.

Mary Lou quickly opened her eyes and with a smile motioned for Sydney to take a seat. "I first want to thank you so much for coming out to our studio to help us with an extremely delicate and difficult situation," Mary Lou began. Sydney smiled back and nodded. "This may be the hardest thing I have ever had to say...". Mary Lou hesitated and said another little prayer before continuing. "I want to apologize to you."

Sydney Monroe's smile turned to shock. She stared at Mary Lou, tossed her light brown hair back and waited for an explanation. Shifting uncomfortably in her chair, Sydney crossed and uncrossed her legs.

"You may not have even noticed, but I must apologize for treating you unfairly and well, poorly. I have always been a huge supporter of Anna, my younger sister. I wanted desperately for her to be a success in this business as a dancer and financially. She of course was the only advanced female teacher for a number of years until you came, and I saw you as a threat to her dominance in the studio. I have always been reluctant to compliment you or support you – I suppose it was to make Anna look better to others. I am truly sorry for my attitude and any remarks I may have made to you or about you. You are a remarkable person, dancer, and teacher. I can not tell you how much I appreciate you and how very hard this is to tell you all of this." Mary Lou stopped, took a huge breath of air, and let her eyelids close briefly.

Sydney was taken back by this whole conversation. This was certainly not what she had expected when she came through the door to this office. She shifted a bit in her chair as she thought about the words she had just heard. "I accept your apology I guess. I don't quite know what to say. This is all so unexpected."

"There's more," Mary Lou proceeded to tell Sydney about Edward's murder – not that she didn't know about it, but there were details that only she and Suzanna had shared with each other because of the calls from the police. Then she told her about Jilli's abduction and what her jailed abductor had said about being hired by someone to get her out of the way. She also explained about the confrontation at the hospital with Jilli's twin Joni and her sister's involvement. "As you can see, we are in a tough situation here. Someone in this studio whether staff or student is responsible for two murder attempts. And I for one want to solve this before someone else gets hurt or killed."

Sydney was drawn in by the story and moved closer to the edge of the desk pondering the implications. Continuing, Mary Lou said, "I need to be able to trust someone. And I need that person to be the eyes and ears around this studio as well as someone who can draw out conversation about this situation. I can't do it. I'm not in a position that anyone will trust me enough to talk about what they saw or heard. But you are. You are a person I trust with this information. I can't even tell Charlotte any of this. Not that I don't trust her, but I just don't know who to trust at this point. Except you. I trust you."

This last statement again took Sydney by surprise. Her blue eyes flashed wide. Sometimes Sydney Monroe appeared to be all eyes. They were large and beautiful and when she opened them wide, it took your breath away.

"Please," Mary Lou pleaded looking deep into those eyes. "I, and the studio, need you and your help."

Sydney nodded slowly. "What do you want me to do?"

Mary Lou explained about the conversations she needed with both Jilli and Joni Wilson. "Why was Jilli targeted? What did they see or hear? What connects them to Edward's murder? It has to be so subtle that they don't even know what or why you are asking. I think you are capable of really getting into people's minds and feelings. That is a real gift. You have that gift."

They agreed to set up daily meetings to supposedly go over schedules for the day. Sydney would try to draw out some information not only from the Wilsons but from the other staff members and the students. She needed to just hang out and be there. Maybe a mention of something would put the pieces of this puzzle together.

"Let me call Jilli right now and ask if you can run over to her apartment for some advice on her students. I'm sure she will be grateful that you are taking over her lessons for a few days. Her apartment is fairly close by," Mary Lou pulled her black telephone book out of the top drawer and scanned down to the "W" page. Grabbing the phone she began to dial the number.

"Jilli? Mary Lou here. How are you doing dear?" There was a pause then she continued. "Sydney Monroe is going to take over your lessons while you recuperate. She just needs a little help that I can't give. Could she stop by in a few minutes to chat about some of your students?" Anther pause. "Thank you. That would be great."

Mary Lou carefully put down the receiver and turned to Sydney with a smile. "She would be happy to meet with you. I think Joni is there taking care of her, so you might be able to talk with both of them. Don't let them know I told you about Joni's presence at the party, but if you tell them about Jilli's attacker's confession that might pull out some interesting tidbits. And thanks…".

Sydney smiled and pondered her next move. What would she say?

XIII.

Jilli Wilson's neighborhood was near the studio. Calm and quiet, large oak and maple trees lined the street creating a shadowy stillness. Jilli shared an apartment with her sister Joni in a quaint stone four-plex tucked back from the street in the middle of the block. Sydney pulled up and parked on the empty street. Only one other car was parked further down. There must be an alley with garages behind the row of apartments Sydney decided. Jilli's building had vines creeping up the front stone giving it the appearance of a small castle. Each of the four apartments displayed stone window boxes jutting out from the framed panes and small rounded bushes clustered along the front of the building.

Inside the heavy door Sydney spotted four mail boxes in the entryway. She pressed the buzzer for the one marked "Wilson" and a short beep let her open the door to the hallway. Jilli and Joni lived up the stairs in the apartment on the right. There was a slight musty odor clinging to the hallway runner centering the stairway as she climbed the short flight.

Joni answered the door, and Sydney realized at that moment how much the two looked alike yet retained their different personalities. Joni's eyes and facial expressions were Jilli's but she wore a pair of faded jeans with colorful embroidery along the pockets and a ruffled flower print shirt that was certainly not Jilli's style at all. Joni turned back and stepped aside allowing Sydney to spot Jilli propped on the couch. Jilli was wearing a silky cream colored robe with just a hint of a lace topped camisole peeking out from the top of the robe. She was barefoot with one long slender tanned foot reaching out to settle on the end of the couch arm. Propped behind her was a satiny plump light moss colored pillow. The bruises on her face were beginning to turn ugly shades of purple circled with a greenish tinge. Strands of honey colored hair draped her shoulders and a strand swept across her cheeks. Sydney had told herself along the way not to mention Jilli's face, and she kept her silence. No gasps of shock only a sweet and comforting smile on her face.

"Thank you so much for seeing me, Jilli. I want to teach your students as best I can. Then you'll feel more confident that everything is going well as you recover." Sydney didn't quite know what she was going to say but the words spilled out easily. The tension was now broken.

Jilli smiled back and patted a spot on the couch for her to sit. Joni stood behind a chair watching – protecting.

Right away Sydney decided she needed to get their attention. "I'm sure you heard the latest about your attacker's confession."

Both Jilli and Joni seemed surprised by the remark. "No? I don't think we've heard anything," Joni quickly took a seat and leaned forward to listen.

"Suzanna gets the latest news from the police and told me an interesting bit of information just this morning before I left for the studio out here." Sydney paused to let that sink in then directed her remarks to Jilli. "I guess someone paid your attacker to kill you. They think it might have been the same person who killed Edward Garrett." Sydney studied both faces and saw the color draining. This was not something either had considered before this moment. This was definitely news to the two of them. "The police feel you were very lucky indeed. You could have been a murder victim. You were not chosen at random as they previously thought. It was a hired murder. I don't know why someone would want to murder you, do you? You must have seen or heard something important."

Jilli quickly glanced at Joni. Joni's face seemed ashen and pale. Her dark tanned face quickly regained its color but Sydney did not miss the initial shock.

"Joni," Jilli moaned and then quieted.

"Jilli was a target, you say?" Joni drew her hand to her face and licked her lips. "I don't know how that can be. Did the police say anything else?"

"I don't know that I got everything but I do know they think that Edward's murder is connected to Jilli's assault." Sydney paused and let the information sink in.

"Jilli wasn't really present when Edward Garrett was murdered. I was," Joni confessed quickly scanning Jilli's startled and frightened face. "Jilli, I ...".

Joni looked down at her bare feet and breathed out heavily.

Sydney tried to look surprised as Jilli addressed her sister. "What did you see, Joni? What did you hear?" Jilli never showed anger, but she began to realize she had been kept in the dark about something important.

"Jilli, I will take care of this," Joni protested in slow and defined words. "I will make sure you are no longer in any danger at all. That's all I can say. I feel terrible that something I may have inadvertently did or said may have caused your attack." Joni rose and then added with added firmness in her voice. "I will take care of this. Trust me."

Jilli cradled her swollen face in her slender finders and let out a slight moan.

"Trust me!" Joni turned quickly and left the room.

The living area of the apartment was cozy – the overstuffed sofa was in the middle of the room with a throw rug of subtle earth tones in front of the couch. The pale toned but slightly textured chair that Joni had just vacated was at an angle facing the couch. Another square chair was positioned on the other side. It had a low back and rounded arms with a fabric that was not in anyway soft nor comfortable in appearance. Behind the couch was a narrow walkway that led to the hall. Sydney assumed the two bedrooms were off the hallway. To the right of the clustered seating group was a small dining area and kitchen separated by an island counter. The dining area had a small round table with high backed carved chairs and a bouquet of roses in the center of the table. Actually as Sydney glanced around the room there were several bouquets of flowers on end tables and window sills. Some were large colorful balls of mums and carnations, others potted plants with cards still sticking up on stems from the dirt. The flowers gave a special fragrant scent to the room – delicate and fresh. A soft sheer curtain was curling in delicate puffs away from the slightly opened window in the corner.

"I'm sorry if I broke any news you didn't know…" Sydney softly placed a hand on Jilli's extended leg. The leg gave a slight flinch.

"I wasn't at the party when Edward was killed," Jilli explained. "Joni was taking my place while I finished up a modeling shoot. I don't know what happened that night, but Joni has had something on her mind ever since that day. Even though we are twins, she didn't share anything about that evening. My working at the studio has kept our lives more separated than in the past. Normally we don't keep secrets. But now it appears that she knows something that put me in danger. And all along I blamed Lee for not protecting me. I thought there was something he could have done differently that would have changed the whole situation. Now it seems I could have been killed, and he wouldn't have been able to stop it even if he tried."

Sydney noticed the 'even if he tried' remark and knew Jilli was still not ready to forgive Lee in her heart. But was she willing to forgive Joni, her own sister, for placing her in this danger? That would remain to be seen. And that would also depend on what Joni actually saw or heard, and what she was now planning to do to 'take care of it'. Maybe Joni was the one they should be concentrating on. But how? Joni wasn't a part of the studio, and it would make it difficult to know what she was going to do.

The two talked briefly about each of Jilli's students and checked over lesson plans then Sydney left for the studio. When she entered the reception area, the music swelled seductively. Eloise with her ear to the phone pointed to Mary Lou's office door as she caught Sydney's eye. Sydney nodded and carried her black program folders into Mary Lou's office.

"Yes, Suzanna, I agree it's really an incredible opportunity for both studios...", Mary Lou waved a hand toward the chair. "Absolutely. This is something that could really bring in a whole new clientele." She paused to listen. "We could pull together the mambo routine. Jilli just called me to say she should be back by Thursday. I'm sure with a touch of make up, no one will even notice the difference in her face. She said the swelling was almost gone and she felt like doing something rather than sitting around feeling sorry for herself." Another pause. "Yes, that certainly is a good sign. I agree. Then we'll meet you at Garcia's around 10:30 on Thursday evening. See you then." She put the phone down.

"So Jilli called after I left her place?" Sydney was somewhat surprised but nodded slightly. Her blue eyes widened as she prepared to fill Mary Lou in on the conversation with Jilli and Joni Wilson.

"So Joni did see or hear something," Mary Lou said flatly.

"She also said she would 'take care of it'. Whatever that means," Sydney repeated. "I think it might be important if Jilli is planning to come back so quickly to let the staff know that Joni was the one present when Edward was killed. Just to be on the safe side."

Mary Lou nodded. Whoever had a hand in this must know that Jilli was the wrong target. But did that mean just the staff? What if it had something to do with a student? Mary Lou considered this as Sydney checked her watch and rose abruptly to teach her first lesson of the day.

Mary Lou poked her head out of her office door and spotted Charlotte seated next to the music system at the end of the small ballroom. The front desk hid the stereo from students waiting in the reception area, so Charlotte's huddled figure was tucked back in the corner with Charlotte leaning in to listen to several pieces of music turned down so as not to distract from lessons going on in the back ballroom. She wore a slim but basic sleeveless dress of beige linen. The sides slit to just above the knees exposing Charlotte's thin but well muscled legs. She had a pair of old slip on canvas shoes that she always wore before lessons to keep her dancer feet from getting too pinched and tired. A dancer's feet could easily become swollen and sore after an eight hour dance day. Charlotte had long ago learned the secrets to preventing foot problems. Comfy canvas shoes during the day was one of those secrets.

Mary Lou scurried across the floor and knelt by Charlotte. "We have the opportunity to dance each week along with the downtown studio at a club in St. Paul called Garcia's."

"I know that club. It attracts mainly Latin dancers from the neighborhood." Charlotte added with a nod as she turned down the music to listen more closely.

"We're going to do one routine each Thursday – Latin of course. The downtown studio will put together two routines. They have twice the staff that we have and some of the newer teachers could really use the extra experience in performance. I told Suzanna we could easily revive the Mambo for this Thursday." Mary Lou explained the new opportunity.

"The 'Mambo of Death'?" Charlotte shook her head with a shudder remembering the last time they had performed that routine was at the party that turned up a dead body at the conclusion.

"Now Charlotte, we can't disregard that routine just because Edward's death happened to coincide with our first performance. It's such a fabulous routine. We have to use it. Besides Jilli will be coming back on Thursday, and it will be easy to rehearse a number everyone is already familiar with. Do you think you could whip up some costumes? We certainly can't wear 'West Side Story' attire for a Latin club."

Charlotte smiled. "I think I can put something together quickly." She nodded. "Yes, I have something in mind."

"Oh, by the way. The police think Jilli's attack was a murder for hire. They think the person who killed Edward Garrett is responsible for Jilli's assault. The intention was not sexual but murder that got muddled." Charlotte sat back in her chair and with her knees pressed tightly together splaying her feet and legs to the side.

"Well, that means they don't know it was Joni Wilson who was at the party and not Jilli...". Charlotte was one person who knew this information as she had been present when Jilli's sisters chatted in the hospital waiting room. "Jilli could still be in danger unless we get this information out."

"I agree," Mary Lou nodded. "I was thinking we need to tell the staff immediately. But also we need to somehow get the news to the students. We don't know

141

right now who might have been involved in both events. It could have been a student. How should we go about doing that without just making an announcement? That might tip someone off that we know the two events are connected."

"Well, my suggestion would be to introduce Joni at the Friday dance party. Anyone thinking Jilli to be a threat would have second thoughts after we introduce the two of them side by side. That would be subtle enough." Charlotte's idea was good. Mary Lou agreed. They would invite Joni to attend the party Friday and make a big thing of introducing her to everyone.

At the end of the evening, Max Krinkie had sauntered off with the students after his lesson for a night cap at a local dance club. The students had a habit of going out after lessons together for a little practice in an actual social situation. Mary Lou had quickly herded the rest of the staff into her small office for a meeting. It was cramped but she was determined to keep this session away from lingering ears. Some students made a habit of waiting around the reception area for as long as they possibly could at the end of the evening. Eloise would keep a watchful eye on those who couldn't seem to leave promptly.

Lee had come in to teach lessons that day and stood in the corner of the office leaning against the wall. His face was somber as he ran his fingers through his soft light brown curls. Charlotte and Becca sat in the chairs reserved for students. Becca let her brown hair drape across her face as she hunched over a bit in the chair. Charlotte sprawled her legs out in front of her with her casual canvas shoes looking very inviting after a long day of dancing. The splits on either side of her lean linen dress opened revealing her legs. Kenneth stood behind Charlotte's chair rolling his shoulders back and forth getting out the kinks of holding a dance position for so long. Sydney held on to the back of Becca's chair for balance and tried to lean back far enough to rest her back on the wall behind her. The atmosphere was quiet.

Mary Lou began by explaining the plan about Garcia's. She told them they would revive the mambo routine for Thursday and that Jilli had called to say she would be back for the performance. Lee's face showed signs of both relief and concern. He seemed to have feelings of being in limbo with Jilli. Guilt and concern and anger all wrapped up in one ugly ball showed as he quietly dealt with all the emotions. His first day back after the stress of Jilli's attack had been a strain for him. The rest of the group whispered bits of comments to each other before Mary Lou continued.

"There is one thing I think I should share with you," she paused as the faces returned to attention. "Jilli Wilson was not in the studio when Edward Garrett was killed. Her twin sister Joni was." No noticeable sign of surprise from the group. Strange.

"How many of you knew Jilli had a twin and that she was here for that party?"

Lee of course raised a hand immediately as did Charlotte. Then Becca, Kenneth, and of course Sydney put up their hands. No one was surprised by the announcement. Mary Lou stopped momentarily to consider. If no one from the staff was unaware of Joni's presence at the party that meant it wasn't one of them who targeted Jilli. They would have known it was Joni instead. Of course she had always hoped her staff hadn't done anything to either Jilli or Edward. Then who? Students? Maybe the downtown staff? She had left them out of the possible equation. Now they would have to be added in.

"Oh, before you all go," Mary Lou added. "Charlotte will be designing new costumes for the women, and men – you wear black pants and black shirts."

The staff practiced the mambo a few times before Jilli's return on Thursday. Jilli had opted not to teach that day but would be in for rehearsal early in the morning. She chatted with Mary Lou as they waited for the rest of the staff to arrive. Mary Lou asked if she could invite Joni to attend the party the next evening. Without explaining the reason for the request, she casually eluded to the idea that the studio would feel better if Jilli were accompanied by someone when coming and going to the studio. Jilli agreed and seemed to accept that explanation without question. The face foundation Jilli wore covered any discoloration from her bruises. She seemed quiet yet happy to be back with other people around. Her expression seemed to show a safeness even when Lee came in and with slight hesitation moved over to the place where Jilli stood to engulf her in his arms. She paused for a moment and then moved in to the embrace and clung to his body burying her head in his chest. And that was that. They were a couple once again. At least for the moment.

Charlotte waltzed in carrying a stuffed garment bag. Unzipping quickly, she pulled out a hanger for each woman containing a slinky black wrap skirt with a scalloped hem, a sequined tube top in black glitter edged in magenta and apple green, and a matching sequined scull cap in black with the same magenta and green edging. The stretchy cap fit tightly on the top of the head allowing the hair to hang down without getting into the face while dancing – at least that was what was supposed to happen. There were "oohs" and "aahs" from the group except for Mary Lou who groaned when she saw the tube tops. She of course was dancing the Mambo as she had at the West Side Story party. The tubes and skirts would look great on the other three women – slender and tall. But on short stubby Mary Lou? Would the outfit make her look just that – short and stubby in comparison?

Charlotte was about five seven with a thin build. Her delicate bone structure was evident in her tiny wrists and ankles. However, in spite of her almost too skinny body, her breasts were full and plump. The tube top would look great on her to accentuate her body assets. With her long fine hair, the cap would be stunning emphasizing her large eyes, slender neck and delicate facial features.

Jilli on the other hand had a perfect model's body. About an inch taller than Charlotte, Jilli was slender but not thin. Every inch of her body was tanned, toned, and exact in proportion to what it should be. Jilli's chest was average and looked perfect with the rest of her body making her the swim suit model that she was. Her long slender hands and fingers moved elegantly as she danced. The flowing honey colored hair would wave softly back from the cap just like

146

a model in a photo shoot when the fan gently swirls the hair away from the face trying to look naturally windblown.

Becca was larger boned yet still slender. An inch shorter than Charlotte, Becca had a thickness throughout her body that showed in her heavy wrists and ankles. Although pregnant, she didn't show any signs yet displaying instead a toned and tight stomach and a flat chest. Her upper body was wider and more muscular more like that of a gymnast. Becca's best features were her large very white teeth and her thick shoulder length sable colored hair. Anyone first meeting Becca was drawn immediately to her smile and then to her luxurious full head of hair.

"Now Mary Lou," Charlotte said in her soothing voice. "You will look just darling in this and the costumes will look flashy under the stage lights at Garcia's. Just what we want. Trust me."

"Trust me," Mary Lou mumbled. "I've heard that one before." She tried on her outfit and it was just as stunning as Charlotte had predicted. "Oh, OK. I guess this will be just fine," Mary Lou added glumly then tried to add a smile. Mary Lou was about a head shorter than the rest and although tiny in her clothing size, her body was ...well rounder and more mature. Nothing could make that hat look good with her short curly head of hair. The tiny curls stuck out all around the edges. Charlotte quickly tucked and poked some of the ends back under the cap edge giving Mary Lou a slightly better look than when she had pulled the hat down over the crown of her head initially. Each of the other two women came over to poke and piece her hair into place and finally in the end, the look was better – not great – but better.

They slowly went through the routine reminding Jilli of all the choreography. Then they put the music on and began staging the routine in all directions. Sometimes when rehearsing a routine, it can cause confusion if it always faces one direction. So they first did the routine toward the wall of mirrors. The costumes flashed and sparkled in the glistening mirror. They turned the routine around facing the teachers' office with no mirrors. After a few missed steps, they finally got it down. Then they moved to the large ballroom and rehearsed toward the back wall storing the sound system. Tiko, a Latin band consisting of several instruments would be playing that evening. So they would not have their practice music – an added worry for some. Instead they would have to dance as the musicians played and to the temp Tiko set for the Mambo. Mary Lou had heard Tiko several times before and promised the tempo would be just perfect.

"Let's carpool to Garcia's tonight so we all get there together," Charlotte suggested. She and Mary Lou were chosen as drivers. They packed up the costumes and began to set up the table for the daily meeting.

Jilli and Lee walked down the hall for a cool drink from the little café at the end of the mall. They walked slowly, talking just briefly. Would their relationship mend? At this point it was hard to tell.

Eloise scurried in and noticed the bright red marking "Garcia's" written across the schedule. Mary Lou was standing at the desk and pointed out the markings she had made.

"We are going to be doing a show every Thursday evening at Garcia's in St. Paul. We need to be there by 10:30, so if you can try to schedule our lessons to end just a bit early on Thursdays, we can use the travel time," Mary Lou explained.

Eloise frowned. Any changes in the schedule meant more shuffling and rescheduling for her. "Schedule change" was never a welcomed phrase to Eloise. She pouted making her puffy cheeks unbecoming and her bright red lips crooked on her lopsided face. Her dyed blond hair was beginning to show dark roots and was even shorter and curlier than Mary Lou's style. With a grunt Eloise plopped herself into her rolling desk chair and stared at the schedule tapping her pencil on the 10:00 time slots. Her usual short and clinging skirt eased up her round legs. "Well, I suppose I could work on this today. You could have given me more time. After all I've been scheduling and rescheduling all week long," she complained in a nasally tone. Her nose always seemed pinched at the bridge giving her voice a phone operator's twang.

"Thank you, dear," Mary Lou said sweetly. "And make sure you check all the schedules for the next few weeks as well. Hopefully this will be a long term show for us. We can always use the business." Eloise made a "Hrumph" sound at the suggestions that the studio could use additional business making her job even busier. Mary Lou wondered how many appointments Eloise turned away by her sour attitude and attempts to lessen her daily work load.

"I might talk to Max Krinkie about joining the staff permanently. Now that Lee is back, I have to admit it was nice to have another male teacher around. Kenneth and Lee would probably like another male to help out with new students. That might make your job a little easier as well," Mary Lou tried to sound positive as she prepared Eloise for changes. Eloise didn't like change. Eloise didn't like much of anything actually.

"And how is that boyfriend of your? Ben isn't it?" Mary Lou was trying especially hard to be nice to a clearly miserable woman.

"What? Oh, Ben? Yes, he's fine. As best he can be," Eloise said not sounding too complimentary. "Ben? Ah, yes, Ben!" Her face began to show signs of thinking. This was an unusual event, Mary Lou thought. Eloise thinking! What could be next?

Mary Lou prepared to leave a bit earlier with Jilli and Lee who were the first ones ready for the trip to Garcia's. Charlotte would have to take Kenneth and Becca along with Sydney. All three were still teaching, and Sydney would be doing one of the downtown studio's routines that evening. Grabbing their costumes, Mary Lou stood at the desk for one last glance at the schedule and to check tomorrow's appointments.

"Jilli, is Joni going to pick you up tonight? Or will you be riding home with Lee?" She glanced over her shoulder at the pair. "I need to keep my eye on you and keep you safe. You are my number one priority," she added.

Lee nodded in agreement. "And mine, too," he was quick to put in.

Jilli blushed under her dark tanned face and turned to smile at Lee. "I will keep you safe. Promise!" Lee whispered.

"Sweet," Eloise muttered under her breath from behind the desk. The glasses perched on her nose began to slide down as she gazed again at the crossed out notes she had made on the schedule. Not satisfied to just erase and rewrite changes to the appointments, Eloise always crossed off and wrote on top or in the margins so people would notice how much work she had done to get any changes in for the day.

As the three walked out to Mary Lou's car, Eloise grabbed a puffy mohair sweater preparing to leave as soon as the last lesson was finished. No use hanging around any longer than need be after all the changes she had made all day. Her oversized hand bag dangled from her arm, and she snatched up the phone to make a call.

Garcia's was located in the middle of a short block in an off downtown area of St. Paul. The air was damp and warm giving the street lights a hazy appearance. The other stores on the block were by now closed – the Mexican grocery store, the real-estate office, and the corner import shop. Garcia's was popular with the local residents from the neighborhood. Small groups stood around outside on the sidewalk as the lively music filtered out to the street.

Mary Lou found a parking spot across the street and the three scampered across the street to the smoky dark club. The dance floor while not huge was larger than the tiny spaces found in most clubs. The customers in this club loved to dance so the floor was a prominent part of the business. Tiko was on a small stage in the front of the club. Mary Lou, Jilli, and Lee found a table out of the way of the smoky air by the back hallway that led to the rest rooms and the back exit.

Milli Mae Carter from the downtown studio was getting ready to start out the show. She and partner Bobby James had an amazing Samba they liked to perform. Milli Mae was a few inches under five feet tall so wore the tallest dance shoes available to give her a little added height. She wore a wrapped skirt in bright pink, yellow and aqua flowers with a matching halter top. On her head was a wrapped headdress in the same bright fabric topped with fruit – bananas, oranges and pineapples just like Carmen Miranda from the old movies. Milli Mae inherited the tiny costume as no one else could possibly fit into it.

Bobby was about five six and built like a powerful wrestler. He was what was known in the dance business as a "lifter". He was so strong that he enjoyed tossing and lifting his partners around giving the audiences – and his partners - added thrills. Milli Mae was one of his favorite partners as her tiny size made her especially easy to throw into the air. This Samba routine was amazing to watch. Milli Mae ended up on his shoulders then wrapped down around his body ending on the floor and then Bobby would swing her around the floor into what was known as a "death drop". It was always a popular routine that no one ever grew tired of watching.

The Samba would be a perfect start to the show. The Garcia patrons would eagerly clear the dance floor and give the dancers space once they saw the amazing moves this couple was performing. That would make the Mambo easier to get into. The stage would already be set for the second number and the fast Mambo was always a popular dance to watch.

Charlotte, Kenneth and Becca hurried in and dropped their bags onto the table in the corner. Charlotte primped a bit and played a bit with Mary Lou's hair as they put their caps on and pulled out their dance shoes. Dance shoes have a soft suede bottom that most dancers will not wear outdoors opting instead to save wear and tear on their shoes for a dance floor. Charlotte's shoes were a Latin style strappy shoe in gold. Jilli always wore a gold Latin sandal with an intricate pattern of thin gold bands wrapping around her foot, and Becca chose a heavier shorter black shoe that gave her more support when she danced. Mary Lou also wore a black Latin sandal with a t-strap up the front stitched with rhinestones. Kenneth stretched out his shoulders as they all watched Milli Mae and Bobby take the floor.

The Samba went quickly with Milli Mae flying around the floor and wrapping up in Bobby's arms to end in a pose that almost toppled her heavy headdress from her head. But she readjusted it before rising from the floor as the crowd cheered loudly.

The Mambo routine was fast with quick footwork and spins from all the dancers. The light was catching the glitter of the caps and tube tops flashing glints of light every time they twirled. The two men were dancing behind the four women. Just as they hit their final pose something unthinkable happened. All four tube tops dropped exposing their breasts. It was quite unexpected and coincidental that it happened at the same time to all four dancers. In a flash all four women quickly upped the tops but the crowd went wild after the first seconds of silent shock. The group quickly exited the floor and scurried to the table to grab their other clothes. Then Charlotte began to giggle and all but Mary Lou hid in the corner laughing uncontrollably. An experience that they would talk about for years to come.

The downtown group was clearly put at a disadvantage having to follow both crowd pleasing performances, but the six couples sauntered to the floor amid claps and cheers for "more!" for a highly charged but mellow Cha Cha. Sydney was one of the twelve dancers. And although the Cha Cha was good, it would never compare to the Mambo. Not after that ending.

Mary Lou sat huddled on one end of the table. There were several groups of students from the studio who had come for the show, so the teachers needed to stay at least for a few dances to make sure all were having a good evening of dancing before leaving. Charlotte was trying to comfort Mary Lou when a waitress scampered in from the exit – outside taking a break from the crowd.

"Call an ambulance!" she yelled. Her dark hair and eyes flashed with fearful shock. "Hurry!" she yelled at the bartender. She was wiping bloody hands on the white apron wrapped around her waist and holding a lit cigarette in her teeth.

Mary Lou and Charlotte ran out the back exit to the dark alley. There was only one light hanging to the side of the door giving a shadowy gloomy feel to the air. Along the other side of the building were several garbage cans and in front of the cans was a person sprawled on the ground. In the darkness Mary Lou and Charlotte crept closer to see a woman lying on her back with her legs splayed at an awkward angle. She wore faded jeans and a bloody shirt. It was Joni Wilson. Mary Lou instinctively squatted next to her and felt for a pulse.

"She's alive," she whispered. "Hurry, get help." Charlotte went to the door but hesitated not wanting to leave Mary Lou alone in the darkness. What if the assailant were still in the alley? She pulled opened the door and yelled for help.

Suzanna, Jilli and Lee popped their heads out to look at what was causing such a stir. Charlotte immediately grabbed Jilli and held her close as Suzanna ran to aid Mary Lou.

"What are you doing out here?" Suzanna hissed when she saw who was lying on the ground. "You know the police will have a field day with this if you are sitting with her in this dark alley."

Mary Lou hadn't thought of the implications of her actions. "This woman needs help," she answered back. "What would you do? Leave her?"

Suzanna knelt down and held Joni's hand. It was only a moment before the paramedics came around the side of the building with a stretcher. Police lights began flashing in the alleyway. Jilli was screaming in a breathy hoarse voice, "No! No!"

Charlotte began to calm her down with her soothing tones. "Was Joni coming to see you in the show?"

"No, she didn't know anything about Garcia's. I only told her I would be at the studio to teach today. That's all," Jilli answered back quickly shaking her head.

Mary Lou and Suzanna listened closely to the short conversation as they watched the paramedics lift Joni's lifeless body to the gurney. Mary Lou looked closely for the source of the blood and saw it was coming from her head. Joni had been hit in the head. And she hadn't known about Jilli dancing at Garcia's. That meant someone else from the studio – or studios – had called her. Where was Joni's car? How had she gotten here?

"Jilli, let's look for Joni's car. She must have driven here some how. Let's try to locate it," Mary Lou said quietly glancing at Charlotte and Suzanna. Lee was standing back behind the group with a look of pain on his face. Mary Lou quickly caught the arm of one of the attendants and asked where Joni would be taken. There was one hospital in downtown St. Paul that would be close.

The group huddling together moved around the alley to the front looking for the small blue car Joni Wilson drove. By now a group of Garcia's patrons were standing out in front watching the flashing lights and ambulance in the middle of the street. The street was not well traveled at this time of night. Mary Lou had easily found a parking spot and there hadn't been even one car that passed them in that few minutes they took to park. Many of the club's customers had walked or had parked earlier in the evening.

"Excuse me," Mary Lou said tapping a woman she had noticed outside when they arrived. "Have you been standing out here for the last few minutes?" The woman nodded her head. Mary Lou continued. "Did you happen to see any cars pass by in that time? It seems pretty quiet along this street this time of night."

The woman thought for a moment and then nodded. "Yes, there was a pick up truck that passed. It was driving very fast toward the highway ramp. That's why I noticed. It came from down that way." She pointed down to the left. "It was light colored. White but very dirty."

"Did you notice the driver?" Mary Lou persisted.

"I think it was a man. But he may have had a passenger. I'm not sure because the driver's side was towards me," the woman squinted as if trying to think. "Someone shouted at him to slow down. That's how I remember it so clearly."

Mary Lou nodded a thank you and then directed the group down toward the left to continue looking for Joni's car. They spotted it around on the side street. Jilli had a set of spare keys in her purse and quickly fished them out to open the door. Everything seemed in order but on the dashboard was a handwritten note on a small scrap of paper. "Garcias". Then there were a few rights and lefts marked – directions.

"I had better get over to the hospital and call my mom," Jilli said weakly. Lee offered to drive her over in Joni's car.

Mary Lou, Suzanna and Charlotte walked slowly back to the club. "Well, we know that Joni must have heard or seen something the night of Edward's murder. And we know that someone from the studio who knew we would be at Garcia's tonight called her to set up a meeting at the same time that we performed." Mary Lou went down the list of things they knew. "Makes us look more guilty doesn't it. Us being right inside during the attack."

Charlotte added, "We were the closest to the exit door and didn't see anyone from the studio going in and out during the show. Of course, we weren't looking for anyone. But I would say that the attacker had to have gone around the back of the building rather than through the exit door."

"True." Mary Lou tried to think back. There was not very much activity in the back corner during the few short minutes they had been there before the show and during the show – they probably would have noticed enough to greet a staff member who passed by. The bathrooms were in the hallway, but the waitress had come back almost immediately after the end of the show. There just wasn't much time there for others to go in and out.

"The Mambo of Death," Charlotte whispered softly as they went back to the club. "Best we not perform it again."

Another trip to the hospital. It was becoming a bad habit. A different hospital, but the same scene. Charlotte and Mary Lou huddled in the corner with Joni and Jilli's mom seated again across from them. Suzanna had volunteered to drive Kenneth and Becca back to the studio. The other sisters were also arriving to wait for any news. The gray commercial carpet on the waiting room floor gave the room a gloomy feel. The wait was once again agonizingly long.

"I think that Joni saw Edward's murder but didn't know it at the time. It took her a while to put all of the picture pieces together. That's why there was such a time gap between Edward's death and Jilli's attack. She must have figured out what had happened and contacted whoever was responsible. But the murderer didn't know it wasn't Jilli. Joni must have spoken to the murder in person. Face to face." Mary Lou chatted quietly to Charlotte letting her mind move from idea to idea. Charlotte nodded.

"But the murderer knew this time that it wasn't Jilli who witnessed the murder," Charlotte added. "They set Joni up by arranging a meeting at Garcia's. Maybe for some sort of payoff. Joni must have decided it was profitable and asked for money in exchange for silence. But why would she feel safe meeting this person knowing what had happened to Jilli?"

"Maybe she thought any accomplice was already in jail. After all, Jilli's attacker is in custody. I think Jilli's attacker really was telling the truth when he said he didn't know who hired him. I think it was a random hire." Mary Lou and Charlotte talked back and forth in low quiet tones so as not to upset any of the Wilson family.

It seemed like a long time. Jilli sat in a chair cradled by Lee and the other sisters patted their mother's hands. Finally a doctor came out. He explained Joni was in a coma but was doing better than they had expected. He said the police would want to speak with them shortly and decided a guard at Joni's door would be best to insure her safety. The family nodded their heads – still worried but a sense of relief clearly visible on all their faces.

"The question is," Mary Lou continued. "Who didn't know before the first attack that Jilli had a twin, but knows now. We didn't tell anyone but our staff. The students were going to meet Joni tomorrow at the dance party. Who on the downtown staff knew about the twins?" Charlotte rolled her eyes back in thought. "And who has a dirty white pick up truck."

Mary Lou got up to stretch her legs and grab a bottle of water from a vending machine she had noticed when they arrived. As she put her dollar into the machine and pressed the button, she noticed the pay phone in the corner. She opened her chilled bottle and put a few coins in the phone slot.

"Suzanna? Thanks for driving my staff home. Sorry for calling so late. I'm at the hospital waiting for any news. I have a favor to ask." Mary Lou had two questions in mind. First, could Suzanna use her connections with the police to get news about Joni and their theories about the incident. Second, did she know who from the downtown staff knew about Jilli being a twin.

"Well, Jilli went right out to your studio when she started her training so she wasn't very close to anyone on our staff. They are of course all concerned, but not really too in tuned to Jilli Wilson's personal life. Of course Sydney Monroe knew. You had her out to the studio when this whole thing began to unfold. Anna? I don't know. Did you say anything to Anna?"

Mary Lou and her sister Anna were usually very close but since Edward's murder, they hadn't really communicated very much. Had she mentioned anything about Joni Wilson? She didn't recall saying anything about the twin. When Sydney's name was mentioned, Mary Lou hoped somehow in the pit of her stomach that Sydney was the one involved. She could still feel the sting of revenge that she had always felt toward Sydney. But after a brief

164

thought in that direction she knew that Sydney had nothing to do with this.

"I know Sydney wasn't involved in any way," Mary Lou said after a hesitation. "I have complete trust in her. Besides she was performing at the time of the attack. We know she was there in Garcia's the entire time. I had Sydney go to the Wilson's apartment to gather information, and Joni would have shown some sort of recognition and maybe fear if she knew Sydney was the murderer of Edward. Joni knows who the murderer was. I am convinced of that fact. No, I don't think that Sydney Monroe has anything to do with this. Anna? I would hope not. I don't remember saying anything to her at all about the twin situation."

"I don't recall any of my staff coming in or going out during the evening before the performance tonight," Suzanna said firmly. "I don't like to feel that they had anything to do with this or the other attacks." Suzanna was a bit short when she recognized the implications Mary Lou was making about someone on her staff. "I'll give you a call first thing in the morning after I've talked to the police." Then she abruptly hung up the phone and Mary Lou was left with a loud dial tone in her ear.

XIV.

The morning paper was unfolded on Mary Lou's breakfast table. Mary Lou was sipping a cup of hot coffee and biting into a piece of toast as she scanned the headlines. "St. Paul Attack Leaves Little Hope For Victim". Mary Lou read the story. It implied strongly that Joni Wilson – unnamed victim in the story – was unconscious and not expected to live. Could this be true? Or were the police feeding the story to the media to save her life?

The phone rang and Suzanna quickly apologized for her shortness the night before. "I know you are trying to solve this because you are a prime suspect in Edward's murder. I'm sorry I was so upset by the thought that someone from my studio could be involved in any way. I promised to help you, and I hope some of what I found out today may make it unravel somehow." Suzanna took a deep breath and told Mary Lou that the police expected Joni would recover. However, she was still in a coma. They wanted anyone involved to feel safe so had asked the media to mention the possibility of no recovery. They needed the person involved to make a mistake. Suzanna had told them about the white pick up but the police had no news or information on the vehicle. They might be checking into Joni's phone records and checking account to see who she had been in contact with recently. The bank account information might tip them off to some sort of a payoff. All of that was up in the air at the moment, but Suzanna might have more to report later today. She would keep Mary Lou informed.

Finishing her breakfast, Mary Lou slipped into a dark navy skirt and scooped neck white blouse then grabbed a cardigan sweater to wrap around her neck. It was warm outside, but the studio was always kept cool. She was the first one to arrive and settled back behind the reception desk to go over the daily schedule. The first message on the answering machine was from Sydney Monroe.

The sweet voice announced she would come out in the morning to teach Jilli's students. She assumed that Jilli would not come in after the Garcia attack on her sister. Mary Lou glanced at Jilli's schedule and decided to call all students to inform them of the exchange lesson. Then she glanced at Lee's schedule and decided to put a call into Max Krinkie. Max had been at Garcia's last night. She saw him lounging around one of the tables filled with students. He would surely understand why she needed him to fill in.

Max Krinkie? She hadn't thought about him. He certainly had been around enough this week to pick up on the fact that Jilli Wilson had a twin. Quiet and always polite, she hadn't given Max much of a thought when they went down the list of who knew what. Yes, Max must have picked up on everything the staff knew. Her heart sank as the thoughts began to flood in. Max with his curly blond halo of hair and easy going smile. So likeable and trustworthy. Or was he?

Eloise plopped her large purse on the counter and stared at Mary Lou seated behind the desk. Mary Lou was suddenly made aware that there was another person trying to get behind the narrow area she was occupying. She mumbled an apology and told Eloise she was trying to arrange today's schedule so Eloise wouldn't have so much work to do. Certainly that explanation would make Eloise relieved. Eloise pursed her lips and considered this for a moment and then allowed Mary Lou to slide out from behind the desk.

"I'll call Max Krinkie to see if he can take Lee's students today and Sydney will be coming in to Jilli's lessons," Mary Lou announced.

Eloise wore a short striped dress and carried a sweater over her arm. The air conditioning could be chilly for someone not engaged in the physical activity of dancing. Eloise usually had a few sweaters hanging around the desk in case it felt cold. She stared up at Mary Lou with her sagging eyes as if she had no clue what Mary Lou had just told her. The buggy appearance of her eyes suddenly made Mary Lou feel sick to her stomach.

With a "why bother" attitude, Mary Lou walked quickly to her office. Her sensible shoes clicked on the wooden dance floor. She hadn't changed yet into her dance shoes and as she settled into her desk chair after closing the door, she slid off her shoes with the crepe soles and propped her feet up on a stack of programs piled next to her desk. Closing her eyes, she said a little whisper of a prayer and grabbed Edward's paperback Bible hidden in her top drawer. "Please, Lord...", she pleaded.

After a few minutes of reading and mumbling Mary Lou picked up the phone and dialed Max. Max worked during the day in the family business – a store across the street at the local shopping mall. He and his brother were the co-owners of the shoe store. No wonder Max loved the studio, Mary Lou always mulled. After a day waiting on customers, the movement and music must feel like a pleasant change. In fact the shoe shop customers were the reason Max had come to the studio in the first place. So many studio students had come in to have their dance shoes fixed or repaired, Max had begun to ask questions about where and why they used these suede soled shoes. That got his curiosity up and he came in to take a lesson himself.

Max's brother answered the phone. "Just a moment, I'll get him," he sighed.

Cheerily, Max answered the phone. Mary Lou told him she needed him tonight to help teach Lee's lessons, and he seemed pleased. She knew he did it not for the money, but for the dancing.

"And hey, Max?" she continued. "I …er…the whole studio really appreciates this."

"No problem," he chirped back.

"By the way," Mary Lou suddenly thought of something. "Did you happen to see anything unusual last night at Garcia's?"

"Like what?" She could almost imagine Max frowning as he asked the question. "Unusual? I don't know quite what you mean. Besides the costumes falling off." He laughed a light subtle giggle. "That was certainly unusual."

"Yes, I guess that would be unusual. I mean anyone leaving suddenly or not being there during the performances. You, know. Something you wouldn't expect."

"Not really," he dragged this out. Was he thinking it through or did he remember something he didn't want to tell? She might have to pursue this line later.

"Well, then see you later." Click.

Charlotte looked drawn and tired today. Her usual lithe body seemed especially gaunt and thin. Everything was taking its toll on her. The same could be said for Mary Lou except that Mary Lou had more energy to solve the situation because she continued to feel like a suspect. That gave her a little more of an adrenalin rush each day as she faced the new challenges.

Charlotte smiled an insincere and plastic smile as she put the tables and chairs together in the small ballroom for the daily meeting. Her mind was elsewhere and it showed in her loose fitting sweater that she fidgeted with pulling it tightly around her body and her usual comfortable canvas shoes that she let dangle off her feet as she slumped in one of the chairs.

Becca also looked tired. Her usual big bright smile was a straight closed line on her freshly scrubbed face. Mary Lou suspected the tiredness was due in part to her pregnancy. Kenneth, face pale and pasty with his dark rimmed glasses creating a stark contrast, tossed his blond hair away from his face as he took quick steps toward the stackable chairs around the table. He carried a pile of programs and pulled out a pencil to check through his lesson plans.

Everyone was sluggish and melancholy throughout the day. Max came in at 6:00 with his typical engaging smile and upbeat attitude. Mary Lou vowed to talk privately with him sometime that evening. There was something he hadn't shared with her, and she was not about to let that slide.

At the end of the evening, Mary Lou slid her arm into Max's and told him she would walk him to his car. The night air was warm and moist in comparison to the air conditioned comfortable studio. They walked a few steps out the door just as Eloise's boyfriend Ben pulled up to the curb in his old rusty junker of a car. He nodded curtly to both of them as they began to stroll across the parking lot. Earlier the lot had been filled with students' and customers' cars, but now it had only a few scattered studio staff cars. It was late and nothing else in the mall would be opened at this time of night. Max walked straight toward a bright yellow pick up. Mary Lou had never noticed what kind of car Max drove, and she began to slowly feel a tingle in her body as they approached the truck.

"Is this yours?" she asked as they passed the long backend. Her mind was quickly thinking "yellow…white" could the witnesses have gotten the color of the truck wrong. They were both light colors. The yellow truck was sparkling and looked almost new.

"So how long have you had this?" Mary Lou said touching the silvery bumper along the backside.

"Oh, maybe a year." Max smiled with pride. "I'd always wanted a truck like this."

"It's so clean and shiny," Mary Lou commented.

"Yeah. I get the special over at the Standard station," he pointed to toward the corner gasoline station. "Every Tuesday you get a free wash with a fill."

"So you get a free wash every Tuesday?" Mary Lou frowned.

"That's right," Max grinned. "Every Tuesday it gets a wash and buff down to keep it looking good all of the time."

Mary Lou knew that the witnesses might have gotten the color of a truck wrong but not the condition. This wasn't the truck they were talking about. They had clearly seen a very dirty truck and this was certainly not that. "I suppose you know a lot about cars and trucks," Mary Lou commented looking around the parking lot.

"Yeah, I guess I do. That blue Mazda over there is Charlotte's," he pointed to a car in the middle of the parking lot. "And that little maroon Datsun is yours," he laughed as he pointed out an older small car a few spaces down from Charlotte's. Then he continued to go around the lot picking out everyone's car.

Eloise came clopping out of the mall door banging it loudly as she headed towards the car occupied by the young faced Ben. Ben hardly noticed, sitting straight forward with a grumpy look on his face. Probably felt he waited too long, thought Mary Lou. Eloise's slip on small heels clipped noisily on the sidewalk as she hefted her large purse around her shoulder to give her a maneuverable position to get into the large long car idling with occasional loud groans.

"And Eloise over there," Max was saying, "drives a short bed white truck. A Toyota, I think."

Mary Lou suddenly came back to life. "What? What did you say about Eloise?"

Max repeated his statement about Eloise's vehicle being a small white truck. "It's old and rusty and she hasn't been driving it ever since Ben has been picking her up every night. But that's what she had BB. Before Ben."

He laughed at his joke and started on about some of the other cars some of the students drove. "Yeah, that silver BMW that David Drexler has…".

But Mary Lou was no longer listening to the car stories. She was instead focusing in on Eloise Parker now inside the car and trying to adjust her body into the seat. Eloise Parker. Could she be the key to this whole thing? It didn't quite seem possible. Eloise didn't even know Edward Garrett that well. In fact she hadn't really been around him at all. She was a student when the studio opened and had only joined the staff recently - just before Edward's death. What could she possibly have against Edward? She certainly couldn't have a grudge against him, could she? For what? Mary Lou's mind was churning a mile a minute as she let Max droan on and on about his love of cars. Yes, Max had known something. But she didn't think he knew this was the piece of information she was looking for. He had it but didn't know it.

"Well, Max." She stopped him from going on. "I must get back inside, but thank you so much for teaching Lee's lessons tonight. I appreciate all that you've done for us in this strange situation. Maybe we can talk sometime about you really teaching – part time of course," she added when he gave her a puzzled look. She gave him an affectionate hug and watched as Ben and Eloise sped noisily toward the parking lot exit. Then she moved toward the mall door.

Once inside she headed toward the reception desk. Charlotte and Kenneth were just getting ready to leave. Charlotte had a large brightly patterned cloth purse thrown over her shoulder. When Mary Lou commented on the bag, Charlotte told her she had designed and sewn it herself.

"You are just so talented!" Mary Lou declared trying to seem normal when inside she was churning with questions about Eloise and her involvement with this whole thing. She nodded pleasantly to the two as they left then quickly grabbed the phone and called Suzanna in the downtown studio. Hopefully she hadn't left yet.

"Yeah, Suzanna," she juggled the phone on her shoulder pressing it tightly in her ear as she pulled opened the file cabinet at her feet with one shoeless toe. "I know who killed Edward and planned the kidnapping of Jilli. I just can't explain why at this time because I can't for the life of me figure that part out."

Suzanna sucked in a large breath of air. "What are you doing? Don't tell me. I know it's dangerous."

Mary Lou pulled out the employee files and paged through until she found Eloise Parker's application for employment. She glanced down at the address. In her mind she was planning to find Eloise's home address and drive by to see if she could spot the truck. When she explained to Suzanna that she had discovered "maybe" the owner of the white truck seen leaving Garcia's, Suzanna began to angrily talk into the phone. "Mary Lou, I know what you plan to do. And you are not...I repeat not going to that house to find that truck. I am going to call the police and let them take care of that. It is way too dangerous. Whoever this person is that you discovered has this truck has killed one person, hired a killer for another, and attempted to kill a third person. Does that sound like a dangerous person to you? I would say so."

Mary Lou stopped and thought for a moment. "OK, Suzanna, you win. But the finding of this truck does not tie this person to any of those three events. We need more evidence. That's what the police will say, and you know it. We need a plan to get more evidence out in the open. I think I know just what we need to do. But we do need the help of the police. Could you ask them to meet me out here so I can go over my idea?"

It was only a few minutes before a police car pulled up to the studio and out popped Suzanna along with two officers who had been working on the Edward Garrett case. One had been the one to initially interview Mary Lou and seeing him again gave her a stomach ache. She opened the door and invited them all into her small office where she explained the details she had just learned from Max Krinkie. One of the officers made a quick call to the station and found out that yes, indeed Eloise Parker did own an older model white pick up truck. While that part of the story seemed to interest the detective, the idea she presented gave the three of them a moment to ponder and soon the plan was beginning to take shape. Mary Lou quickly made a call to Jilli Wilson.

"Jilli, I know it is late, but I need to stop by your apartment for a moment. I have information on who might have arranged your kidnapping and attacked Joni." Well that piqued Jilli's interest, and she immediately invited Mary Lou to stop by.

Mary Lou slid into a parking spot in front of Jilli and Joni's apartment. The door promptly as she reached the front door. Lee was there propping open the door and looking curious.

The three of them settled into the comfortable living room. One small light was on in the corner casting a few long shadows across the room. Jilli was curled up on the couch with a comforter around her, Lee was seated next to her and Mary Lou took a chair across from them. Mary Lou explained that she had found the owner of the white truck seen at Garcia's but they needed more evidence to tie the owner to the other events including Edward Garrett's murder. Jilli and Lee looked curiously at each other when Mary Lou told them Eloise owned the truck. "I need to help me flush out Eloise," Mary Lou explained turning toward Jilli.

"What can I do?" Jilli asked.

"Eloise feels safe right now because the paper reported that Joni was in a coma and not expected to recover. She feels safe that the information that Joni has – whatever that might be – is sure not to be repeated. So we need to make her feel that Joni has recovered and is going to tell the police what she knows. Tomorrow I need you to dress up as Joni."

Jilli and Lee both looked confused and a bit shocked. Joni was targeted because she was trying to play Jilli and found out something she shouldn't have. Now Jilli was going to play Joni. That was a switch.

"You need to dress like Joni," Mary Lou explained recognizing almost at once when she made that statement that Jilli didn't know that the two of them dressed differently. Mary Lou would have to explain that Joni tended to dress in a more old fashioned – no, "traditional" manner with flowers and ruffles rather than the chic single toned pieces chosen by Jilli. "Pick an outfit from Joni's closet," Mary Lou suggested. Then she explained that they would have to wrap her head in bandages so it would appear she had a head injury and maybe use some make up to give her eyes a blackened appearance. Jilli nodded understanding the look she needed to pull this off.

The police would escort Jilli to the studio tomorrow at exactly 1:15 pm. They needed to make sure that Eloise was at work before Jilli made her appearance. Lee would have to come in earlier as if he were working his regular schedule and tell Eloise that Jilli wasn't feeling well and needed Sydney to take her schedule for a few days. Lee nodded – understanding the importance of his part. Then he would have to seem surprised when "Joni" made her appearance.

The next morning, Mary Lou was nervous. She arrived at the studio earlier than usual and parked herself in her office. Pulling the now worn paperback Bible from the

180

top desk drawer, she paged through a few favorite passages before peeking out to see Eloise arrive as usual and slide behind the reception desk.   She poked her head out for a moment trying to appear as if she needed a program for a lesson and in the process waved to Eloise so she would know that Mary Lou was already in the studio. Lee walked in and greeted Eloise and then pointing to Jilli's schedule asked Eloise if she could call Sydney to take Jilli's schedule again. "She's not feeling too well today," he explained. Eloise smiled and nodded with a knowing look. Then Lee walked into the teacher's office.

A man walked in and with a few long strides reached the reception desk. He flashed his badge and then announced he needed to speak with Mary Lou Smith. At first Eloise seemed uneasy but when he explained that he needed Mary Lou, Eloise relaxed and with a broad but crooked smile told him he could find Mary Lou in her office right across the small dance studio floor. Eloise waited – poised – as he crossed the floor and knocked on the office door. Then she smiled. Quietly she picked up the front desk phone and whispered a few sentences into the receiver.

Mary Lou and the detective sat huddled around the speaker on Mary Lou's desk. They had placed a bugging device near the phone and were now listening in on Eloise's conversation. "Ben, the police are hear to question Mary Lou. I think she's their main suspect. Joni Wilson must have died." Click the phone hung up. Eloise then remembered she needed to call Sydney Monroe. After reaching her, she made a few quick lines on the appointment sheet and stood up to peak over the desk top toward Mary Lou's office. The officer had looked stern and grim faced when asking for Mary Lou – "Miss Mary Lou Smith" he had said in official sounding tones.

Suddenly, Jilli – "Joni Wilson" appeared at the studio door with an officer holding her elbow and helping her move slowly and unsteadily into the reception area. "Mary Lou Smith?" the officer asked Eloise whose face suddenly turned pale and sickly. Joni was the last person she ever expected to see here in the studio. Not now – not walking – not talking. Jilli made a point to stare at Eloise as the two of them passed on their way to Mary Lou's office. The glare made Eloise sink into the chair. When they closed the door to the office, Eloise quickly grabbed the phone and dialed Ben.

"Ben, Ben," she whispered excitedly. "Joni Wilson just walked in with an officer. You gotta come get me. Quickly! Now! We have to get out of here and as far away as possible. She's gonna tell them everything she saw. She's gonna tell them she saw me put the pills into the punch. Hurry, Ben."

The four stood around the speaker listening intently to the whole conversation. Quickly the officer dialed his phone. "Pick up the guy. She called him and they are about to run." Then he called a second officer who was waiting outside the door, and he moved in quickly to arrest Eloise Parker as she tried to gather up her things. Her face was angry as Mary Lou and Jilli stepped out into the ballroom. With her hands secured behind her back, Eloise glared at the two.

"What did you tell them? Did you tell them you saw me put the pills into the punch cup sitting on the desk? I thought you were dead... or almost dead. You were still in a coma the paper said. Everyone said. How did you get here?" Eloise's voice spit out the words with furry and anger.

Jilli Wilson looked confused at first and then suddenly she began to assume her character. "Yes, I told them everything," she declared boldly.

"You didn't even know what you saw at first. It was a few weeks before you contacted me with your blackmail scheme. Did you tell them about that? Did you

183

tell them that you tried to get money out of me? I paid you the first payment and then realized you would take everything I had. Ben told me you would. He knew what kind of person you were. We didn't know you weren't Jilli Wilson and had to hire someone to get rid of Jilli. That's when you came back and asked for more. More! You wanted so much more because of that little mistake. How was I to know you were a twin…". Eloise mumbled on thinking she was accusing Joni of crimes – that she was getting Joni Wilson into just as much trouble.

At that point, Jilli couldn't go on with the charade and broke down in tears. Lee was just inside the teacher's office door and came rushing out to support her as she collapsed to the floor.

"Oh my God! You are Jilli. You didn't know any of this, did you? You tricked me." Eloise's puffy face twisted into a painful recognition of what had just happened. She had confessed all without anyone else telling the police any of the details. She closed her eyes and hung her head.

"Eloise," Mary Lou managed to whisper. "Why did you kill Edward Garrett?"

Eloise raised her head sharply. "I wasn't trying to kill Edward Garrett. I was trying to get back at you. You!

You treated me so poorly always yelling and telling me what I was doing wrong. I wanted to make you sick. I never meant to kill anyone, just make you **sick**."

"Well, that you did. That you did. You made me really sick," Mary Lou whispered back. Edward had never been the intended target. She, Mary Lou Smith had been the one who had made the enemy. She was the one who was suppose to drink the punch laced with pills – pills that Eloise had just scooped up and thrown into the cup for a little revenge. Revenge for Mary Lou's sour, mean treatment of an employee. It had all happened because Mary Lou had treated someone badly. Jilli kidnapped, raped, and almost killed. Joni beaten into a coma. And Edward. Edward Garrett dead all because Mary Lou hadn't treated someone else fairly.

The officer lead Eloise out to the waiting police car. Ben had been apprehended and the house searched for evidence. The officer had reported that Ben had been arrested several time for robbery and assault in the past. They showed Mary Lou the last arrest picture of Ben – his pasty face sneering as he turned from front to side. His dark hair was oily and slicked back from his face with one lone hair hanging across his forehead. Would Eloise have done these things without Ben and his influence? Who knows. The police had done some digging into Eloise's past after the conversation last evening suggesting she might be a viable suspect. They found some interesting things that they had decided to look into. Her first husband had mysteriously died in a car accident after he left her for a younger woman. Would they find Eloise was somehow responsible for the accident? Maybe.

Jilli Wilson slowly removed the bandages from around her head, and Lee gently wiped the black makeup from around her eyes. She was slumped into a chair in the reception area smoothing out the ruffled white skirt that didn't quite feel comfortable. She and Lee would go over to the hospital to see if there was any improvement in Joni's condition before spending a few hours with Jilli's family explaining the events of the day. The answers they wanted would be bittersweet. It was good they found the person responsible – not so good that Joni was now labeled a blackmailer and that blackmail scheme was the reason for Jilli's attack. If Joni had gone to the police with her story, none of the attacks would have occurred. But she was greedy. The police would find the deposit of Eloise's money in Joni's bank account. The connections would be made.

Mambo Basic:

Man's part: Step side with the left foot (Slow count), Rock back with the right foot (Quick count), Replace weight forward to the left foot (Quick count), Step side with the right foot (Slow count), Rock forward with the left foot (Quick count), replace weight to right foot (Quick count). Repeat.

Lady's part: Step side with the right foot (Slow count), Rock forward with the left foot (Quick count), replace weight to right foot (Quick count), Step side with the left foot (Slow count), Rock back with the right foot (Quick count), Replace weight forward to the left foot (Quick count). Repeat.